Seaside Surprises

The Seaside Hunters

by Stacy Claflin

http://www.stacyclaflin.com

To receive book updates from the author, sign up here.
http://bit.ly/1ONrfMw

One

JAKE HUNTER LEANED BACK IN his chair, grateful to have a minute to sit. Sweat beaded on his forehead, and his shirt stuck to his back. He would have pulled on the bottom of it to fan himself, but his muscles ached too much to bother.

He looked at the door. No one was coming, but it was only a matter of time. The little shop had been busy all day, not giving him a break until that moment.

Jake rubbed his knee, knowing he couldn't keep up much longer. It was the height of tourist season, and his parents needed to hire some employees.

Usually, they took care of everything and he never saw them this time of year, except when he helped out in the shop. With his younger sister's recent passing, they refused to leave their house. Jake was heartbroken over losing Sophia to cancer, but he knew how much harder it had to be to lose a child—their only daughter. So, he worked the extra hours without complaint.

Perhaps he needed to take it upon himself to hire an

assistant or two. If nothing else, that might pull their parents out of the house, if not their depression.

What about *his* time of mourning? He was the one who had taken care of Sophia the when she was sick. Sure, there had been nurses coming and going, doing what he couldn't, but he had given up his life for a couple years. Not that he was complaining. He wouldn't have traded a minute, especially now that she was gone.

His throat formed a lump, thinking about Sophia. He remembered her so full of life, dreaming big dreams. Even with what life had handed her, she had refused to let it get the best of her. At the end, she had comforted everyone else, telling them not to be bitter because she wasn't. She was glad for the life and family she had been given. After having spent so much time with her, he knew she meant every word of it.

If she had been there with him right then, Sophia would have given him a break. She would have either sent him to go get lunch or she would have brought some to him. She might have even made it her mission to find a couple employees to help Jake out.

Out of all their brothers, she was closest to Jake. It had been strange in a way, because she, as the only girl, was the clear favorite, and Jake was the least favorite of all the kids. That was why he was stuck running the shop alone in the wake of the family's tragedy.

The cancer had not only taken their sister, but nearly destroyed the entire family. Jake wasn't sure they would ever recover.

The bell above the door sounded, and Jake cleared his throat and blinked his misty eyes. A group of teenage boys came in, punching each other and laughing. They headed for the back where the unhealthiest treats were stocked.

When Jake was sure that none of them could see him, he wiped his eyes and cleared his throat again. He had to learn to stop thinking about Sophia when he was out in public, or at least working.

He looked up at the mirror on the corner of the ceiling closest to the group of kids. They were too quiet. Jake narrowed his eyes. It looked like one of them was sliding candy into his pocket.

Jake groaned. Why wouldn't his parents get cameras? With as many thieving punks that came through the doors, the cameras would more than pay for themselves. He pushed the chair back and stood, preparing himself for the confrontation, pushing aside his aches and grief.

The mirror showed another jerk stuffing something into his shorts. Anger burned in Jake's gut, and he rushed over to the kids.

"What do you think you're doing?" he demanded.

"Just looking at snacks," said a guy with slicked back hair and a shirt slung over his shoulder.

"It doesn't look that way to me." Jake indicated toward the mirror.

"Oh?" asked Slick. "And how are you going to prove

anything?"

"Ever heard of security cameras?" Jake stepped closer.

The boys made eye contact and laughed.

"What's so funny?"

"You don't have any of those," said another. He
pulled back some of his long, blonde hair behind his ear
and narrowed his green eyes at Jake. "Otherwise you
wouldn't have those ugly mirrors."

"You don't know that. The mirrors help me catch
people and the cameras provide proof," Jake lied. He
raised his eyebrows, staring at each one of them.

Blondie rolled his eyes. "We know 'cause some
dudes came out with a bunch of candy from right under
your nose and your *high tech cameras.*"

The boys all laughed and gave each other high-fives.

"Get out," Jake said through gritted teeth. "But first
hand over the candy."

"Try to get it," said a short, stocky kid. "Think you
can?"

Jake's nostrils flared. "Hand it over before I call the
police."

"Over a candy bar?"

"Theft is theft." Jake pulled out his cell phone and
slid his finger across the screen.

"Dude, I think he's really going to call the cops,"
said Shorty, eyes widening.

"Who cares?" asked Blondie. "What are the cops at

this lame, little beach town going to do to us? It's not like we're taking anything expensive. Come on." He headed for the door.

Jake grabbed his arm. "You're not going anywhere until you return the merchandise."

Blondie shoved Jake. "Let go of me before I have my dad sue you for harassment."

"Big words for a little thief. Hand over the candy."

Jake felt hands wrap around his shoulders and then he felt the pain of a shelf corner jamming into his back. Another set of hands shoved him, and Jake fell to the ground, hitting his head. His already-sore knee twisted.

"Run!" yelled Slick, and they all headed for the door. But not before Jake held up his phone and snapped a picture. He turned it around and looked at the image. All he got was half of the back of Blondie's head.

He shook his head. So much for that. Jake got up and ran for the door, pushing it open. He could still see the kids running down toward the beach.

"You thieves better not come back," he shouted. For all the good that would do. Jake rubbed his back and his head. He was going to tell his parents he was done unless they made serious changes, and soon.

He went to the register and sat. Maybe he should just close shop for the day. That would show his parents he was serious.

The bell rang and a pretty brunette walked in by

herself. Jake did a double take for that fact alone. During tourist season, everyone traveled in packs.

She looked about his age, early-twenties, and had long, wavy hair that nearly reached her waist. Despite the heat, she had on skinny jeans and a long-sleeved sweater.

As the door closed behind her, she pulled her dark sunglasses to the top of her head and looked around the store. She had gorgeous, almond-shaped eyes. Most of the girls coming in looked like they hoped to run into a Hollywood producer who would hire them on the spot for the next blockbuster. This girl had a natural beauty, and that made Jake curious.

He got up and walked over to her. "Can I help you?"

Looking startled, she turned to him. "I just need a few things. I don't think I'll need any help." She crinkled her cute, button nose as she gazed to the back of the store.

"Are you sure? I know where everything is."

She turned back to him, her bright green eyes studying him. "I'm not even sure what I need yet."

"No one else is here, so you may as well take advantage of my expertise. Once the next rush hits, I'll be stuck at the register."

One side of her full lips curled down. "I'll risk it, but thanks."

"Okay, but if you do need any help, you know

where I am."

She nodded, not moving her feet.

Jake studied her lightly freckled face. She seemed to have a lot on her mind, very much unlike every other girl running into the shop. People came to town so they could forget their worries and the locals were all busy with their own businesses that time of year.

"Just give me a shout if you need anything." He went back around the counter, this time, leaning against it rather than sitting, so he could watch her. There was a sadness about her that made him curious. Jake wanted to know more, but she obviously didn't want to talk.

She switched her purse to the other shoulder while still standing in the same spot. Finally, she went toward the far side, near the back where they had some refrigerated goods. He continued to watch her in the mirrors along the ceiling. The girl stopped and looked at a few things, but didn't even pick anything up.

The door opened, forcing Jake to focus on ten new people in the store. He recognized a few of them who had been coming in regularly since the previous weekend. Another group came in, followed by another. The store was soon as packed as it had been all day.

He kept his eye out for the sad, pretty girl, but she didn't come to the register. He couldn't find her in the mirrors either, so she must have not found what she needed and slipped away when he was busy with customers.

People came in and out for the next half hour before the store emptied again. He looked at the clock. It was only a quarter past three. Where were his brothers when he needed them?

The brunette came around an aisle, holding a few basic items. Where had she been hiding?

He smiled. "You found what you need. Sure I can't help with anything else?"

She shook her head, the sunglasses falling over her forehead. "I'm good." She pushed the glasses back and dumped everything on the counter.

Jake rang up the microwave dinner, milk, coffee, and cold cereal. He told her the total and waited for her to hand him the card so he could find out her name. Instead, she gave him some cash.

"No card? You're not the typical tourist."

"Nope." She looked around, looking eager to get out of the shop.

Not that he could blame her. Jake couldn't wait for the shop to close. "Where are you staying?"

"Around."

"There are a lot of places to eat around here. You don't need to eat this." He held up the TV dinner before putting it into the bag.

She gave him a sad look. "I'm not a tourist."

"Do you live around here? I thought I knew all the locals." He did, actually, but he didn't want to put her on the spot.

She took the bag and stepped away from the counter. "Keep the change."

"But it's over five dollars."

"Get yourself a latte. I gotta go. Sorry." She hurried toward the door, sliding her glasses back onto her nose.

Shaking his head, Jake watched as she left the store. If she wanted to lay low, she had come to the wrong town.

Two

Tiffany Saunders, soon to be Petosa again, threw the plastic bag onto the hotel bed alongside her suitcases. The food needed to go into the fridge, but she was too tired to move. She had paid too much for it. Everything had been overpriced and then she had told that cashier to keep the change.

She kicked off her shoes and then peeled off the sticky clothes, putting on shorts and camisole. Then she put the food away and went out to the deck. At least she had a view of the water. Tiffany walked over to the railing and leaned against it, watching the waves of the Pacific Ocean bounce around.

Seagulls flew about, chasing each other and otherwise just enjoying the beautiful day. If only she could enjoy it. As relaxing as it was, she couldn't help looking below to see if she was being followed.

As far as she knew, Trent didn't have a clue where she was. Just a week earlier, she had packed up what she could as he slept. Then she had taken the packet her grandpa had given her so she could start a new life.

Not only was she going to find someplace new to live, she was going to take on a new identity. It should have been something fun. A brand new start, especially given what she was leaving behind, but the past didn't let go so easily.

The tall, handsome cashier had been so nice, but she couldn't bring herself to tell him anything about herself. Tiffany had tried to say her new name, but it wouldn't roll off her tongue. She *was* Tiffany, sometimes Tiff, but never anything else. Now she had to get used to an entirely different identity.

Would this new life give her the change she so desperately needed? Even if it did, was that what she really wanted? She was scared—no, terrified—to make the same mistake again.

She hadn't known Trent's true nature before they married. It was hard to remember, but he used to hold open doors for her, lavish her with gifts and praise, and even sing songs to and about her.

What had happened to that man? Had it all been a farce? A ploy to trick her into marriage?

Tiffany had been scared of Trent's temper for too long, believing his lies. If she would have been more attentive, a better cook, kept the house up… then he wouldn't have said such cruel things to her.

A couple weeks ago, she realized the way Trent acted had nothing to do with her. And more importantly, he would never change. He couldn't let go of his anger, and it grew worse with time.

One evening when he had been screaming profanities as usual, she thought he would get tired of lambasting her, grab his beer, and fall asleep in front of a game. But then he picked up a vase and threw it at her head, barely missing, hitting a shelf instead. If she hadn't moved out of the way….

She hadn't been able to go to sleep that night. Couldn't even bring herself to go into the bedroom where she heard Trent snoring. Instead, she sat on the couch, barely paying attention to the television.

The next day, he came home with a big box of candy, a dozen roses, and an expensive bottle of wine. Tiffany hadn't even been able to look him in the eye. He worked long hours the next few days, giving her the space she needed, but then when the weekend came, he returned. Along with his temper.

He screamed at her for hours after she burned some beans. She stood there, taking it silently as usual. Once he got it out of his system, he would grab a beer and fall asleep in front of a movie.

Only, he hadn't. Trent grabbed her shirt and shoved her into the wall, pinning her against it. With his face barely an inch away from hers, he screamed insults and profanities, spraying spittle in her eyes. He yanked her toward him, and then slammed her back into the wall, smacking her head off it.

Terror ran through her, but she managed to steady her voice before speaking. "Trent, you need to stop."

His eyes narrowed. "Stop? Are you joking? I'm only beginning." He took a fistful of her hair and bashed her head into the wall.

"Please," Tiffany begged.

"You're pathetic." He threw her against the refrigerator. "Get out of my sight."

That was when Tiffany realized that if she didn't leave soon, she might only get out in a body bag. She scrambled to her feet, grabbed her purse, and drove straight to her grandpa's house.

He contacted his friends, and together they helped her with the money and even a new identity.

His sad eyes broke her heart. "If I was a younger man, I would stand up to him for you. The best gift I can give you is to get you a fresh start."

He had some connections that helped her take on her late grandma's identity. The social security number had never been reissued to anyone else, and he had given her a new birth certificate with her grandma's name, but Tiffany's birth year.

She hadn't asked how he had managed to get that. Knowing his connections to the mafia, she was better off without the knowledge.

Tiffany blinked a few times, coming back to the present. She went to her suitcase and pulled out the packet, finding the birth certificate, and looked it over.

Would she ever get used to having a new name?

Trent certainly hadn't had any nicknames for her, unless she counted the name calling. There was no way she was going to own any of those. They belonged to him.

What was Trent doing? He had to have been going crazy. Not only had she left without a word, or even a trace, but now he was left with no one to scream at or control.

Tiffany wanted to have kids, but looking back, she knew it was better that it hadn't happened. It almost had, actually, but she had had a miscarriage, more than likely from the stress. Trent had become even worse the short time she was pregnant, and Tiffany never dreamed that would have been possible.

She shook her head, trying to clear the memories, and then shoved the packet back into the suitcase. It didn't matter. Tiffany wasn't going to waste another minute on him. Trent had taken up too much of her life for too long, and he didn't deserve any more of her thoughts.

The new cell phone rang. Even though she knew it could be only one person, she checked the caller ID.

"Hi, Grandpa."

"Honey, how are you? Have you found somewhere to settle yet?"

"No. I'm just passing through a tourist trap for the night."

"Is it nice?"

"Can't beat the view." She walked back out to the deck.

"Go out tonight and have some fun."

Tiffany sighed. "I need to rest before I hit the road in the morning."

"You need to make friends again. He cut you off from everyone."

"I have friends."

"Oh? Is that why Trent's the only one looking for you?"

"He's looking?" Tiffany's heart sank.

"You expected otherwise?"

"I hope he hasn't turned on you."

"It's not me you need to be concerned about. Just take care of yourself and don't worry too much. He's still here in town, and he doesn't know what kind of car you're driving, where you're headed, or anything. It's driving him crazy. He told me as much, before I had to hang up on him. I don't know how you put up with him for so long. I can't take five minutes over the phone."

"That's one reason I was sick so much. I've been healthy since leaving."

"That's what your old grandpa likes to hear. Now get out there and try to make a friend."

"Right."

"I'd best be going. Got my poker game tonight. I

need to win back last night's losses from Frankie."

"Tell the boys I said hi."

"Will do. The offer still stands to send one of their grandsons to protect you."

"I'm fine. It's like you said, Trent doesn't know where to look. That's all the protection I need. You've given me everything else."

"Get out before going to bed, hon. Bars are full of people looking for someone to talk to."

"They're also full of guys looking for something I have no interest in right now."

"Just tell 'em you're gay. That's all the rage these days."

Tiffany shook her head. "Goodnight, Grandpa."

"'Night, dear. Give a holler if you need to."

She ended the call and then tossed the phone to the bed without leaving the deck. The sound of the waves beckoned her, so she leaned against the railing again, losing herself.

After a while, she thought about what her grandpa had said. She wasn't going to a bar, but she wasn't against a little window shopping. Then she could at least tell him she had mingled with others. He would ask.

Tiffany went inside the room, showered, and put on fresh clothes. Fresh, but wrinkled. They still smelled of the detergent that Trent made her use. She hated it, but getting screamed at over soap wasn't worth it.

At first, she fought for herself, but after several unsuccessful arguments, she gave in, finding life easier if she gave Trent his way. He never backed down. Never. He'd kept her up until past two in the morning countless times, yelling and threatening her until she finally gave him his way out of pure exhaustion.

He thought everyone would give him what he wanted as long as he broke them down. That was how he had "worked" his way to nearly the top of his company. Only the CEO held more power than him, and even so, it was only a matter of time before one of them gave in and quit their power struggle. Tiffany's money was on Trent. The word 'no' was only a challenge to him.

Whenever Trent wanted a raise, he would storm into the CEO's office, demanding it. Trent always walked away with his raise. Every time.

It was the same with his family. When he wanted something from his parents or siblings, he threw a temper tantrum until he got it. They always told him what a jerk he was, but Trent didn't care. He had gotten his way.

Tiffany put on the final touches of eyeliner and examined herself. Her long, dark hair was already starting to curl. She hadn't had the space to pack her flat iron. Oh well, it wasn't like she was trying to impress anyone.

There was no way she was getting involved with a relationship anytime soon.

The dark circles remained under her eyes from so

many late nights. It had been typical of Trent to work late and then wake her to yell about whatever had pissed him off that day. By the time he was done, he was snoring away, but Tiffany would be so wound up with stress that she couldn't get herself back to sleep. That was probably the exact thing Trent wanted.

Perhaps some retail therapy would get her to stop thinking about him.

She grabbed her purse and made her way down to the hotel lobby. At the front desk, she asked the clerk where good shops were.

Three

∿

JAKE LOCKED THE STORE, SHOOING away some tourists who wanted in. "There's no such thing as a twenty-four hour shop around here. This is a beach town, ladies."

One of the girls pouted, giving him puppy-dog eyes. "Please."

"Sorry. I've already closed the register for the night." Not that he couldn't open it again, but he wasn't going to. He needed a break after such a long and tiring day. During the off-season, working all day wasn't so bad. It was the kind of town where he could leave the store for a few minutes and nobody would bother anything. Tourist season was a different beast altogether.

Puppy-Dog Eyes switched from sad to a big smile. "You're cute. Are you a model?" She twisted a strand of her hair around a finger.

"Yeah, you're so buff," said a redhead. She reached for his arm.

Jake stepped away, barely missing her touch. "Don't try to butter me up. The store is locked."

She pouted. "I'm not. You should be on magazine covers, though." She looked him up and down, looking hungry. "Got plans for tonight?"

"Actually, I do. But if you make your way to the beach, you'll find all kinds of available men."

"Fine. They probably have pop, anyway. We don't need yours." She stuck her nose up.

Jake chuckled. "That's right. You don't."

The girls scampered off, trying to get into another shop, which was also closing.

He put the shop key into his pocket and made his way to the quieter part of town where the locals tended to hang out. It would be nice to grab a beer and talk with some guys before heading home to his parents' house to discuss business.

Everything was packed. The tourists must have figured out where the good food was. It was always a matter of time. Even though everyone made the effort to point the tourists closer to the beach, they always managed to overrun Jake's favorite places.

But it was what paid the bills year round.

The Robertson's deli didn't look busy, and all of a sudden the "Oceanic," a large sandwich overflowing with fresh shrimp and tasty veggies, sounded delicious. Jake's stomach rumbled. He went in and ordered an extra-large sandwich with a side of chips.

When he walked over to the tables, Jake stopped in his tracks. The pretty brunette from earlier sat at a table eating a bagel. She was looking at her phone, and she was wearing something different—more seasonally appropriate.

Normally, he didn't take any interest in the tourists, but this one had him curious. Why was she alone? And why did she look so sad? Perhaps his curiosity was because of his own underlying sadness about Sophia, his beautiful sister taken too soon.

He walked to her table. "Didn't want the frozen dinner?"

She looked up. It took her a second to recognize him. "Oh, uh, yeah. I'll have that later."

"Mind if I sit? It's pretty busy in here." There were two empty tables next to hers, but he wasn't going to bring that up.

"Sure."

Jake tried to read her, but couldn't tell if she was just being nice, or if she really didn't mind his company.

He sat down. "I'm Jake Hunter. I've lived in Kittle Falls my entire life. You'd be surprised how glamorous it is."

Her lip twitched, but she didn't even crack a smile.

"So, what's your name?"

Her gorgeous, green eyes widened, and then she paused. "It's Elena."

"Pretty. It suits you."

Her face turned bright red.

"Sorry. I didn't mean to embarrass you."

"It's okay." Elena looked away.

Jake frowned. Did she not like him, or just want to be left alone? "What brings you to Kittle Falls?"

She turned back toward him, her expression remaining serious. "I'm just…. Well, I'm making a fresh start."

That made sense. "So you decided to come here of all places?" he asked.

"Just passing through."

Disappointment washed through him. Why? He had just met her. "How long will you be staying?"

She shrugged, taking a sip of her drink.

"If you'd like to see the sights only the locals know about, I'd be happy to show you what this place really has to offer."

"Really? Like what?"

"Well, not much, truthfully." He hadn't expected her to take an interest in a tour.

She looked confused, and rightfully so.

Jake raised an eyebrow. "But I do owe you a latte."

"You do?"

"I've got your five dollars, remember?"

"Oh, that. I told you to keep it."

"And I want to spend it on you."

Elena looked skeptical. "Do you woo all the tourists with coffee?"

"You're the first, actually."

She sat taller. "I suppose there's no harm in that. So, how long have you worked in the store?"

"Since I was in diapers."

Elena's eyes widened.

Jake laughed—a bit louder than he meant to. "Sorry. My parents own the shop, and it's been my second home for as long as I can remember."

"So, you've worked there your whole life?"

"I took a couple years off. My parents can't work now, so I'm back."

"Why? Are they retired?"

"They're in mourning. We all are, actually."

"Oh. I'm sorry. Who passed away?"

"My sister."

She put her hands over her mouth. "That's terrible. I'm so sorry."

Jake cleared his throat. "She was ready to go. She had been sick a long time." That was probably not the topic to discuss with a girl he'd just met. Sure, Sophia had been his life for the last two years, but Elena wouldn't want to talk about death. "You don't know how long you'll be staying?" he asked.

"Not long. This isn't a vacation, unfortunately."

"That's not something I hear often around here. What made you stop here?"

She looked uncomfortable. "I was just tired, and I saw a sign for a hotel."

"You must be on a road trip. I've always wanted to go on one. Is it fun?"

"Not by myself."

"Oh." Jake bit into his sandwich. He needed to find something to ask her that didn't make her uncomfortable or shut down. So far, he hadn't found anything other than a tour of the boring part of town. It didn't help that he hadn't had a girlfriend, or even a date, in a couple years.

They finished their food in silence. She didn't look eager to get away, but he wasn't keeping her engaged in conversation either.

"Are you ready for that latte?" he asked. "Or we could have ice cream instead. There's a shop not too far away that's said to be the best in Cali."

"Is it?"

"I wouldn't know. I haven't tried every ice cream parlor in the state."

"Oh."

Dang it. That was supposed to be funny. "All kidding aside, it *is* a lot better than anything from the store. They make it fresh."

Her eyes lit up. "Really? I've never had fresh ice cream."

"You have to try it."

Jake gathered their trash and threw it away. As they walked down the street, a football flew through the air, heading right for Elena's head.

"Watch out!" Jake said.

Elena turned to him, looking confused.

He jumped in front of the ball just before it

smacked her in the face. It fell to the ground as Jake crashed into a newspaper and magazine stand. A corner dug into his skin as he put his arms out to catch himself. A stack of entertainment magazines flew onto the ground.

"Nice block." Dimitri, the stand owner, held out his hand and helped Jake up.

"Thanks." Jake laughed, though he was embarrassed. He dusted himself off and turned to Elena, who was picking up the fallen magazines.

She handed the stack to Dimitri. "I'll let you organize these. I'm not sure how you had them." She turned to Jake. "Are you okay?"

"I'm fine." His side was burning, but he wasn't going to let on. "Just glad to have kept the football from you."

"Stupid tourists," Dimitri said, and then looked at Elena. "No offense."

"None taken." She seemed to be holding back a smile.

A short, stocky teen in a Cowboys jersey ran up to them. "Can I get my ball back?"

"Watch where you throw it," Dimitri said, glaring at the kid. "Next time you might not get it back." He then said something in Russian to him, not that the boy had any clue what it was. Jake was pretty sure he was either swearing or telling the kid off. Everyone knew to keep the tourists happy, so it was better if he didn't know what Dimitri was saying.

Jake tossed the ball at him.

The kid caught it and ran off.

"Are you sure you're all right?" Elena asked. "You're bleeding."

"I am?" Jake felt his side, and sure enough, his shirt was ripped and he could feel warm liquid.

"You need bandages? Dimitri has bandages." He dug through a box behind the magazines and held up a first aid kit.

Elena snatched it. "Let me take care of that."

"It's just a scratch," Jake said. "I'll handle it."

"No. Let me." She reached for his shirt.

He was used to taking care of Sophia, not having someone take care of him. Elena put her hand against his side and chills ran down his back. Maybe having her help wasn't so bad.

"Do you have a garbage bin?" she asked Dimitri.

"Of course."

Elena handed him the bloody pile and taped some gauze to Jake's side. "I can't do anything about your shirt, but I did get all the sand out of your gash."

"Now I owe you ice cream more than ever."

"I think I should buy you one. You saved my face—literally."

Four

WHEN THEY STEPPED INTO THE ice cream shop, Tiffany looked down at her hand. It was covered in Jake's blood. "I'd better wash up."

"Do you want to pick out a flavor first?" Jake asked.

"Surprise me."

"But I don't know what you like."

Tiffany shrugged. "I'm not picky. How could I complain about free ice cream?"

"Any allergies?"

"Nope. Go crazy." She went into the bathroom and washed her hands several times until all the blood came off. She couldn't believe that Jake had injured himself to protect her. Trent would have shoved her out of the way, giving *her* a gash before he would have risked hurting himself. Or he wouldn't have bothered saving her at all, and she'd have come away with a broken nose. Before he belittled her for being such an easy target.

Tiffany glared at her reflection. Why couldn't she stop thinking about Trent? She had obviously stayed with him too long—he wouldn't even leave her thoughts when she had an extremely handsome guy giving her attention.

She thought of Jake's big, beautiful brown eyes that sparkled when he smiled. His nine o'clock shadow only added to his charm.

It was too bad that Tiffany wasn't looking for a boyfriend, because he would've been perfect. Well, not perfect. She'd learned the hard way that no one was perfect. She wasn't going to stick around to find out what was wrong with Jake.

Tiffany would get her ice cream and then get out of town the next morning, never looking back. Jake would forget all about her as soon as she left anyway. There were plenty of pretty girls running around. At least she could honestly tell her grandpa that she had spent some time with a real, live human.

Tiffany looked herself over to make sure she didn't have any more blood on her, but everything looked good. She left the bathroom and found Jake sitting at a table by the large picture window, holding two ice cream cones. Butterflies danced in her stomach as she watched him looking out the window.

Jake had a gorgeous profile, and he looked thoughtful. Even though she'd barely just met him, from what she could tell, he appeared to have a gentle strength about him. Not a scary strength. If she was ever going to open up to someone again, it would have to be someone like him.

Would she ever be ready? She rubbed a sore spot near her shoulder. Her physical bruises hadn't even healed yet. The emotional ones would take a lot longer.

Tiffany held her breath as she looked Jake over. A strange mixture of feelings ran through her. Part of her begged to give Jake a chance. Maybe he could help to heal Tiffany's hurts. On the other hand, whatever his faults were, they could possibly just add to her wounds. The other part of her wanted to run out the door, and never give him a chance to hurt her.

"It's just ice cream," she whispered to herself. She walked up to the table and cleared her throat.

Jake grinned when he saw her, and held up a cone. Her insides melted a little. Jake was even more handsome when he smiled. The skin around his eyes crinkled just so, and the brown sparkled.

Tiffany went over to the other chair and sat. She tried to look at the ice cream, but couldn't help looking past to Jake.

"I got chocolate chip mint and blueberry. Take your pick." He moved them back and forth, distracting her from his beautiful face.

Both looked delicious, but she found herself more interested in getting to know him than tasting either flavor. "Which do you want?" she asked.

"Nope. You choose." Jake's eyes twinkled as he moved them closer to her.

Looking the cones over, she picked the blue one. It reminded her of the ocean. Green made her think of the backyard of the home she had left.

"Good choice." Jake handed her the cone with blue ice cream.

Tiffany raised an eyebrow.

"Mint would have been an equally good choice." He grinned, further softening her toward him. "These are my two favorite flavors. You would have been happy with either one. Trust me."

Tiffany looked away to regain her bearings, and took a taste. It melted in her mouth. "This is really good!" She turned back to him, seeing how excited he was that she liked it.

"See? Best in the state."

She couldn't help smiling. They ate in a comfortable silence, watching the activity outside. People ran by, chasing each other, squealing, while others strolled by, usually holding someone's hand. It was obvious that the majority of the people were on vacation.

She thought back to her last vacation. It hadn't technically been a vacation. It was her honeymoon. Since then, Trent had spent all of his vacation days at work, earning overtime pay and bonuses. Anger burned in her chest. Why had she stayed with him so long? Given so much up for him? What a waste.

Eager to have a family, she had married him right out of high school. It has angered Grandpa. Now she could see why. And to make matters worse, he was the one paying for her escape.

Grandpa had raised Tiffany after her parents had died when she was young. As much as she had appreciated and loved him for his sacrifices—dealing with her in her teen years had been nothing other than a sacrifice—she had longed to be a part of a *family*. That's what she thought Trent would give her.

Maybe family wasn't meant to be for her. It was for others. She'd made her mistake, and now she was going to be in her mid-twenties soon. Most of the friends she'd had growing up still hadn't even married. They were smart, and families were for them—not her. She had so much baggage now, she would be better off staying away from marriage.

She was angry with Trent for everything he had put her through, but she was even more upset with herself for putting up with it for so long. She should have taken off the first time he called her a name, but she thought that he was legitimately angry with him. Plus, he had said sorry with flowers and candy later.

Tiffany also had her pride to deal with, not wanting to hear *I told you*. Everyone told her it was dumb to marry so young. Her friends begged her to get out and live life before settling down. But she had been so desperate for a family that she ignored everyone.

He went to college and she worked hard to pay the bills while his parents covered his schooling. She had to do all of the cooking and cleaning because his grades were more important than him doing anything around the apartment. Then after he got his job, and they got a house, he still wouldn't lift a finger. He said his job was more important than hers and that he deserved to rest at home, going as far as saying it was her job to make sure he could rest in peace.

She had wanted to make it work, but she hadn't realized that it wasn't possible. He didn't want the *marriage* to work. He only wanted her to serve and praise him.

He had continued to put her down and tell her that all their problems were her fault. He'd even gone as far as saying that because her parents were dead she didn't know how a marriage was supposed to work. For a while, she had believed his lies, but then one day she finally realized that he was full of it.

"Is the ice cream okay?"

Tiffany turned to Jake. She had almost forgotten he was there. She blinked, bringing herself back to reality. "It's the best I've ever tasted." She didn't sound convincing, but she meant it. She had to get Trent out of her mind. He was out of her life, and she needed to act like it. She had a gorgeous guy who actually seemed interested in her sitting next to her.

"You look tired. Want me to walk you to your hotel?" Jake asked.

"Sorry I'm not more talkative. I have a lot on my

mind. I'm being rude."

"No, you're not. It's not a problem. You make nice company either way."

She smiled. Why hadn't she met Jake when she was eighteen?

He cleared the table and threw away the garbage. "Let me take you to the hotel. Which one are you staying at?"

She put her hands to her face. "I can't remember."

"No worries. What does it look like?"

"It was the tallest one. At least, I think so."

"Was it Ocean Heights?"

"Yeah. I think that's it. That sounds familiar, at least."

As they walked back to her hotel, Jake talked about the various things to do. It almost seemed like he wanted her to stay longer. Why would he want that? Couldn't he see how damaged she was? He was better off staying as far away from her as possible. She would probably destroy him.

When they got to the lobby, he asked if she was okay getting to her room on her own.

She stared at him for a moment. Did he want her to invite him up?

He smiled, easing her fears. "I had a great time, Elena, but I need to get back to my parents. I usually check in right after closing the shop."

Tiffany let out a sigh of relief. So he didn't want in

her room. "Thanks so much for the ice cream. It was fun."

"My pleasure. How long are you staying in town?"

"Like I said, just passing through."

Jake's lips curved down. "You're not even staying even another day? I'd love to show you more sights—my treat." He was so cute the way he begged with his eyes.

Tiffany considered staying, but if she spent more time with Jake, she wouldn't want to move on from Kittle Falls. She needed to get as far away from Trent as possible, and this wasn't nearly close to that. She frowned. "I'm sorry. I can't stay. I wish I could, though."

He shifted his weight from one foot to another. His beautiful face looked so disappointed. "If you pass through again, you know where the shop is. Stop in and say hi."

Tiffany forced a smile. The longer she stared into his eyes, harder it was to say goodbye. But she had to. "I will. Thanks again. Bye."

"Have a wonderful life, Elena." He pretended to tip a hat that wasn't there.

She nearly laughed, but covered it, and gave a little wave before turning for the elevators. He was adorable and charming—everything she didn't need right now.

When Tiffany got to her room, she went back to the deck to watch the water. A smile slid onto her face as she thought about the date—no, outing—with Jake. But it wasn't long before her thoughts drifted back to Trent.

It felt so good to be relaxed and out of that stressful environment. She would never get those years back, but hopefully she could at least get herself back.

Tiffany scooted over to the corner of the deck where some sunlight was shining and closed her eyes, letting the rays warm her. This was the life. Even though she was so high up, she could still hear the sounds of the beach. Listening to the waves was going to lull her to sleep soon.

She opened her eyes and went back into the room, ready for a good night's sleep. Her muscles had never felt so relaxed, at least not since she had said her vows.

As Tiffany sank into the ultra-soft bed, she invited sweet sleep to take over.

Five

"WHERE HAVE YOU BEEN, SON?"

Jake took a deep breath. He hadn't even closed the front door, and already the questions began. "Aren't I allowed to have a life?" He closed the door and sat on the couch across from his parents, each in their own recliner.

"Did you run into a friend?" asked his mom.

"You could say that." He rubbed his side.

"Was it Benny? I heard he was coming back to town."

"No, Dad. Don't worry about it. I got the shop closed down and went out. That's all. Speaking of the shop, we're making enough to hire help."

"Not this again," said his mom. "We don't want anyone outside of our family."

"Then you two need to help me out. I can't keep going like this. You're going to work me into an early grave."

"How dare you use that expression in our house?"

His dad narrowed his eyes.

"It's the truth. I can't keep it up. Not during the tourist season, anyway. I understand you're in mourning—who understands more than me? I was the one at her side, caring for her. My heart will never again be whole. But if you can't step it up at the shop, you leave me no other choice except to hire someone."

His mom stood up. "You wouldn't do that to us. We said only family."

"So, you'll start working again?" Jake asked.

She shook her head. "I can't. Not now."

"You know, if you get busy with the shop, you'll find it easier to deal with life. You won't be holed up here, thinking of nothing other than our loss."

"Don't tell me how to live my life, Jake. Just be a good son and keep working our business. It's what sustains us."

Jake ran his hands through his hair, tempted to pull some out. "You need to understand something. I'm not doing this anymore. I agreed to work from open until close to give you some time to mourn. It was never meant to be permanent."

"What do you expect us to do?" asked his dad.

"Something. Honestly, I'm at the point where I don't care. I can either open the shop later or close it early. I'll give you eight hours. Which eight do you want?"

"That'll ruin us," his mom said. "You could do that

in the off season, but now? You've lost your mind."

"Then you either need to hire out, work some hours yourselves, or call in some other family members. I'll give you guys until tomorrow to figure this out. One more long day of work, and then I'm *done*."

His dad shook his head. "Kids these days are so rude."

"Kid? I'm twenty-three, Dad. At least I've stayed around. You act like I do nothing for you, yet I've done more than any of the others. You know it." Jake got up and stormed out of the house. He could hear them inside arguing.

Jake probably should have felt bad, but he couldn't. He was tired of letting his parents call the shots. It was one thing to take care of his sister—that was something he had wanted to do. They all knew she had little time left and he had wanted to be there for her. This though, working the shop alone, that was too much, and they had to face the fact that they were taking advantage of him because he was the only son left in town.

If he was smart, he would figure out where he wanted to go and leave. He walked down the street, careful to avoid people. He didn't want to talk with anyone. After he calmed down, his mind went back to Elena.

Even though he was disappointed she was leaving town, he was glad to have run into her. She had shown him that there's more to life than just busting his butt being a good son when he wasn't even appreciated.

That was a lot for one pretty girl and just an afternoon, but it was the kick in the pants he needed.

Before long, he found himself at a secluded part of the beach. He sat on the sand and watched the waves crash onto the shore. In the distance, surfers took advantage of them.

Jake thought of his time with Elena. Why hadn't he at least gotten her number? Or even a last name? Then he could at least find her online. The more he thought about her, the more he wanted to get to know her. There was a lot more to her than met the eye. That much he could tell.

No stranger to heartache, he could tell she had some herself. What it was, he would probably never know, especially since he had been so stupid. He pulled out his phone and opened the app to his profile. He searched for "Elena." The chances of finding her were low. There were probably thousands upon thousands of Elenas out there and he didn't know where she came from or where she was going.

"Hey there, Jake. What are you doing here?" Dimitri sat next to Jake.

Jake looked over. "I could ask you the same thing."

"I can't bear the tourists any longer. Hey, that reminds me." He dug into his pockets. "My brother and I chased down those jerks who stole your candy. We heard you yelling at them, and went after them. Got the candy back." Dimitri pulled the candy out.

Jake took it. He could feel it half-melted underneath the wrapper. "Thanks, I think."

"Sorry you can't resell it, but we told them to spread that word that your stuff isn't free. So, where's the pretty girl?"

"Probably on the road by now."

"Bummer. You would've made a nice couple."

"You know how it goes with tourists." Jake shrugged as if it didn't matter.

"Did you at least get her number?" Dimitri asked.

"I'm not ready for anything serious."

"You're nothing but serious. A pretty girl like that would do you good."

"Tell that to my parents. They want me to work a thousand hours a week."

"Call your brothers and tell them to get their butts down here. Remember when you all used to take turns with the shifts?"

"That was years ago. Everyone else has their careers. I'm the only one left."

"Then you go somewhere."

"Where?" Jake asked.

"Follow the girl."

Jake laughed. "Right. I just met her. She's just another tourist."

"Really? I saw the way you looked at her."

"Was it that obvious?"

"Dimitri knows love."

"It's not love when you just meet someone."

"Ah, but it can be. You had the look. I still see it."

"Then you see wrong." He slid the phone into his pocket. "What am I going to do about my parents?"

"Good question. What do you think?"

Jake groaned. "You know what I think."

"Then make a decision and stick to it."

"I told them they have to figure it out tomorrow. But they don't get it."

"No, they don't. It's not fair that they expect you to work all those hours with no help."

"It works out to more than fourteen hours when you count clean up and getting ready before opening."

"Dimitri knows. I see you come and go."

"How many hours do you work?"

"I have my brothers who help me."

"Of course you do." Jake pulled out his phone again and scrolled to his own brothers, tempted to give one a call. What would they do? Jump up and leave their various jobs to come back home?

"You going to call one of yours?"

He put the phone back into his pocket. "No. I'm going to give my parents a day like I said. If they haven't figured something out, I'm going to tell them which eight hours I'll work and let them deal with the rest."

Dimitri patted Jake's shoulder. "Good for you. Now about that girl. What's her name?"

Jake stood, dusting sand off his shorts. "See you in the morning, Dimitri."

Six

TIFFANY THREW HER LAST BAG into the trunk, slammed it shut, and got into the driver's seat. She dug through her handbag until she found her key chain—at the bottom, of course. She stuck the key in and turned. A clicking sound came from the front of the car.

"Oh, come on. Not now." She turned it harder. More clicking.

She hit the steering wheel. Her grandpa had checked into the car before giving it to her. One of his buddies who was supposed to know about cars had looked it over.

Maybe it was something simple. Something any guy would know. What would Grandpa look for if he was here?

Tiffany got out and looked under the car for a leak. There were no puddles or drips. She opened the door and popped the hood. Nothing was smoking or steaming, and as far as she could tell, nothing was broken or out of place.

She closed the hood and started the ignition again. *Click, click, click.*

It had to work. The car had been running just fine when she drove it the day before. She turned the key several more times with the same result.

What now? She leaned her head against the seat, sighing. After a minute, she called her grandpa.

He had her check various things, and to add to her frustration, she didn't know what most of them were.

"Well, honey. It sounds like you're going to have to find a mechanic. Tell me you're at least in a decent neighborhood."

"Yeah, it's a cute, little tourist trap. It could have broken down in worse places."

"Okay. Here's what you're going to. Find a mechanic and then get me on the phone. I'm not going to let them take advantage of you. Then once it's fixed, call me again. I'm going to pay for it out of different funds. No using the money I gave you. That's for your starting over. Understand?"

"Yes, Grandpa."

"When can I expect to hear from you?"

Tiffany's stomach rumbled. She had been going to hit the first drive through she came across. "Maybe an hour. I need some breakfast first."

"Okay. Take care."

"Bye, Grandpa."

Where would she eat? Tiffany had slept through the

hotel's continental breakfast, so that was out. She went back inside and asked about mechanics at the front desk. There was one in town. One.

"He might be booked for today. Do you want to check back in?" asked the middle-aged lady behind the desk.

"Not really. I'll take my chances."

"I can't guarantee you'll get your room back. You got one of the best views in the place."

Tiffany set her keys on the desk. "You really think he's going to be full?"

"Usually is this time of year. You'd be surprised how many people don't check their cars out before going on vacation."

"My grandfather had it checked out," she snapped.

"I didn't mean anything against you."

"Sure you didn't. Why aren't there more auto shops around here?"

"Guess nobody wants to give Bobby competition."

Tiffany dug through her purse and pulled out her wallet. "Fine. Book me for another night." She counted some cash, and then handed it to the lady. "I could use a day off from driving anyway."

"Thank you. Have a wonderful day." She gave her the key card and then turned around.

"Wonderful. Yeah, right."

Tiffany made her way to where the auto shop was. Sure enough, it was full of cars.

She went in and explained everything to the tat-tooed guy behind the counter.

"We can tow it this afternoon, but I can't say if we'll actually get to it today. Depends on how all the other cars go. If they're all easy, no problem. We'll fix yours. Otherwise, it could be tomorrow afternoon. Maybe later. It's hard to say."

Another day? "Fine. Whatever you have to do. Oh, and my grandpa wants you to talk to him before you do anything."

"Where's he?"

"You'll have to call him."

"Add his info to the paperwork." He shoved a clip-board at her and moved to the next customer.

Tiffany filled everything out and then gave it back to him. Her stomach rumbled, but she ignored it. She needed to get back to her car and take out everything of value.

Once that was taken care of, she was exhausted on top of hungry.

Even though she had a setback, she was away from Trent and would never have to deal with him again. She was free, even with her car broken down.

Unable to ignore her hunger, Tiffany headed for the part of town Jake had shown her.

"Hey, Miss!"

She turned around and saw the guy from the news-stand. "Oh, hi. How are you?"

"Dimitri's surprised to see you. Weren't you heading out of town?"

"Change of plans."

He raised an eyebrow. "Oh?"

"Yep. Maybe I'll see you around." She walked away. The last thing she needed was to make friends. Once her car was fixed, she would be out of there. She needed to find a decent sized town—a city would be even better—where she could settle down unnoticed. No friends along the way.

She found a little dive to grab a bite. It was somewhat busy which meant the food had to be decent, but not so busy that she would have to wait even longer to eat. Tiffany ate and then decided to make her way to the beach. She kicked off her sandals and carried them, allowing her feet to sink into the soft, warm sand. It slid between her toes and she wiggled them.

Kids ran past, squealing and screaming. Some guys about her age tossed a Frisbee not far away. Plenty of other tourists did their own thing, and none of them paid her any attention. She was glad to be around people, but not needing to interact with anyone.

Her phone rang, breaking the moment. She didn't even have to look. It was her grandpa—who else had the number? Tiffany walked toward the water and answered. "Hi, Grandpa."

Warm water splashed over her feet and up to her ankles.

"How come you didn't call me? Did you get your car in?"

"They're not even going to get to it today. I'm stuck here until at least tomorrow."

"I still want to talk to them."

"They have your number."

"Make sure they call me."

"I will."

"No, Tiff. I'm serious. Vinny checked it out. There shouldn't be anything wrong with it. Nothing."

"Grandpa, I know. You think I want to be here? I just wanted to travel straight through. It makes my skin crawl that I'm not on the move. I keep expecting to turn around and find Trent."

"He's still up here. He's been asking around about you. I know, because everyone wants to know where you are. I'm holding to the story that you must have gotten sick of his ugly mug and took off in the middle of the night."

"If he comes to you, be careful."

"He knows better than to mess with me. If anyone knows the reach of my resources, it's him."

"That's what worries me. If he catches you alone, Grandpa..."

"I can handle a punk kid."

"But that's the thing. He's not a punk kid. He's—"

"Tiff, don't worry about me. I've made it over sixty years because I have brains as well as muscle. Now enough about that lowlife. I've put some extra money in your account. I want you to enjoy yourself while you have some down time. Get a massage and a manicure or whatever that town has to offer."

"Oh, Grandpa. I don't—"

"No excuses. Trent never let you do anything like that."

Tiffany sighed. "Okay. I'll see what they have."

"You'd better. If not, I'm going down there myself to give you a massage and paint your nails. You probably won't like it."

She laughed. "Point taken. Thanks, Grandpa."

They said their goodbyes and she slid the phone back into her handbag. What would she do without him? She hated moving so far from him, but in order to get away from Trent, she had no other choice.

She walked along the shore, kicking water up her legs and keeping her eyes open for a nail salon. The warm sand and water slowly soothed her frayed nerves. Before long, she felt relaxed instead of irritated.

A group of kids ran by, each carrying an ice cream cone. One was blue, and that reminded her of her date with Jake the night before. Maybe being stuck here wouldn't be such a bad thing, after all.

Seven

THE STORE FINALLY HIT ANOTHER lull. Jake went outside and took a deep breath. There was nothing like the fresh ocean air, especially on long days like this one…and every day during the tourist season.

"Jake, buddy. How goes it?"

He turned to see Dimitri. "How do you manage to be everywhere?"

"I wish. Guess who I saw this morning."

"I'm really not in the mood for games."

"A beautiful lady."

"Oh? Do you have a date?"

Dimitri gave him a slight shove. "No. I'm talking about the one you love."

"Would you keep your voice down? I don't love her. We had a nice time last night. That's it. Besides, she's probably already gone."

"No, she's not." Dimitri shook his head.

"What do you mean?"

"She changed her plans. I spoke with her myself."

Jake's heart leaped into his throat.

"Do you think a handsome shop clerk changed her mind…or heart?" Dimitri's eyes sparkled.

"What else did she say?"

"Not a lot. She was in a rush."

Jake slouched. "She hasn't stopped by the shop, so I doubt her staying has to do with me."

Dimitri raised an eyebrow. "The pretty lady had all night to think about you. She decided not to leave. You should find her. Maybe she's playing hard to get."

"Not telling me she's still in town is more than hard to get. It's nearly impossible. Thanks for the heads up, though."

A group of teens went into the shop.

"Gotta go. See you later, Dimitri."

"Find the girl."

Jake waved him off and went inside. Was it possible that Elena had stayed because of him? His heart fluttered and his face warmed. At least he knew which hotel she was at, so he stood a chance at finding her if she didn't stop by the shop. Although if she didn't come by, that probably meant she didn't want to see him.

His mind raced as he dealt with customers the rest of the day. Somehow the day actually flew by. Again he was exhausted from another long day. His muscles ached as he locked up. At least it was his last long day. It was time to find out which shift his parents wanted him to take the next day.

Or...was it time to look for Elena? Some of his soreness melted away at the thought of finding her. If nothing else, his parents would sweat it out while waiting for him to return home. He wasn't going to change his mind.

Jake made his way back to the hotel. He searched the lobby and little hotel shops for her, but didn't see her. She could have been anywhere. Had Dimitri just been playing a joke on Jake? Or maybe Elena had changed her mind and left town anyway. What did his friend know?

Could she have gone back to the shop or for more ice cream? She might have not wanted to bother him while he was working. He headed that way, picking up his pace. He scanned the crowds. Aside from being prettier than most, she would have blended in being average height and with long hair. Most every female tourist from age four to forty had long hair this year.

He passed the auto shop and noticed how full it was. Could that have been why she had stayed in town? Had she had car trouble? If she was on a road trip, any number of things could go wrong. Wear and tear could do a lot of damage to a vehicle.

Perhaps he could still find Elena and talk her into another ice cream cone. Or would that be too boring? There was usually a concert near the beach in the evenings. Maybe she would be interested in that.

He peeked in all the stores he passed by, not seeing

her in any. Was looking for her a dumb idea? She hadn't even bothered to go where she knew he would be. She probably had a boyfriend—how could someone so gorgeous not? Elena had probably called him to keep her company while she waited on her car.

Bobby. That was it. He could swing by the auto shop and find out if Bobby had seen her. It was a long shot, but that was all he had.

He turned back that way and found Bobby sweeping inside.

"Jake, yo. Long time no see. How's your family?"

"We're getting by."

"Sorry about your sister, man. I know you guys were close." He rubbed his stubble, giving his old friend a sympathetic look.

"Yeah, thanks. That's not why I stopped by, though."

"Car troubles?" Bobby looked hopeful.

Jake shook his head. "I'd have to have a car for that. No, I have a question about—"

"Dude, you need a car. I can get you one cheap. What's your price range?"

"Bobby, you're not listening. I need to know if you've seen someone. A tourist."

"You're going to have to be a little more specific than that, yo."

Jake described Elena. "Have you seen her?"

Bobby's lips curved upward. "The girl with the

bright green eyes. She's hot. You know her?"

"I asked what *you* know about her."

Bobby gave Jake a knowing look. "Not much. She was anxious to get the car in, but I go in order. No exceptions."

"That's all you got? You can't give me more?"

"No idea what's up with her car, but I'll be lucky to get to it by the end of tomorrow after the day I've had today. Even if tomorrow's better...I still doubt it." Bobby rubbed one of the tattoos on his arm.

Jake felt hopeful. She might be around a little longer. "Did she mention a boyfriend or anything?"

Bobby grinned, showing some gold teeth. "You really like her. I can try to find more out for you, dude. Oh, wait. I'm supposed to talk to her old man—or was it her gramps?—before I do anything to the car. So, sounds like no boyfriend to me."

"When you see her, can you text me?"

"Want me to hold her hostage so you can rescue her?"

Jake snorted. "Maybe. Depends if I can leave the shop or not. Can you at least put in a good word for me?"

"You bet. Hey, I gotta finish up here or I'm never getting home tonight."

"Don't let me keep you," Jake said. "Oh, and thanks, Bobby."

Bobby waved him off.

Jake ran his hands through his hair. What was it about that sad girl that had him so eager to find her? Though he was exhausted, he would walk through the entire town if that was what it took to find her. He scanned the crowds across the street. She could be anywhere, including in her hotel room.

He walked toward the crowd as he continued to look for her. Everyone was in groups or coupled off, and since she was in town by herself, he looked for anyone by themselves. He made his way to the beach and the boardwalk. At least it was a nice night. The sun felt comforting as it beat on his back.

"Jake!" someone called from behind. "Jake, there you are."

He turned around to see his cousin, Dan, running toward him. His eyes were wide and he looked pale. "What's the matter?"

Dan dropped his surfboard. It sent sand flying. "It's your dad, Jake."

Jake's chest tightened. "What about him?"

"I'm sorry. He collapsed. An ambulance is on its way. May actually be there by now. Come on." Dan gave Jake a hug and then grabbed his board. "If we hurry, we can get there before he's taken away."

Eight

TIFFANY MADE HER WAY BACK to the hotel. She'd just had a full-body massage followed by a mani-pedi, and it left her feeling relaxed all over.

She was about to step off the sidewalk when an ambulance whizzed by, whipping her hair into her face. Tiffany pulled the strands that stuck to her eyelashes, and crossed the street. She couldn't take her eyes off her fingers or toes as she walked. It had been so long since they'd had any color, and her big toes even had cute palm trees decorating them.

Curious about her car, she went the long way into the lobby so she could go through the parking lot. The car was gone from its spot. Maybe they had even gotten to it early. She was too relaxed to drive, so she was glad to have the excuse to stay in the hotel another night.

When Tiffany got to her room, she moved her luggage from the bed and made herself comfortable. She grabbed the remote and turned on the TV, but she was more interested in her nails.

Her eyes grew heavy. Was she supposed to call Grandpa? Or was it only if she knew anything about the car? Probably best to call him either way.

Tiffany pulled her phone from her pocket and called his number. It rang and then went to voice mail. He almost never let it go to the message when she called. Worried about her safety because of Trent, he kept himself on call in case she needed him.

She left a message letting him know she'd taken his advice to get the manicure, and then she put the phone on the closest nightstand. Tiffany fell asleep before she had time to focus on what was playing on TV.

She woke up to the sound of gunfire. Everything was dark except for the glow of the TV screen. Some old western played on the screen. That had to have been what woken her.

Tiffany released a breath she hadn't realized she was holding. She slid off the bed and went into the bathroom. Her hair stuck out in different directions, but she noticed her face looked better—her skin was clearing up and the dark circles were fading underneath her eyes. Some of the lines on her face were fading also. Grandpa had said they were from stress. Tiffany had blown him off, but maybe he was right.

She looked younger just from getting away from Trent. Between living in fear of his temper and him interrupting her sleep so often, the stress had really taken its toll.

Looking into her green eyes, she struck a deal with herself. If the car wasn't going to be ready before lunch the next day, she would get a facial. Then she would probably feel like a million bucks—or at least like a normal human being.

She finished getting ready for bed, and then went to the nightstand to check her phone. No missed calls or texts. Her stomach twisted in a knot. What if Trent had decided to question Grandpa about her whereabouts? Sure, he was one of the toughest old guys she knew, but did he really stand a chance against someone like Trent?

What if Trent brought some friends along with him to see what he knew about Tiffany's whereabouts? It was after two in the morning. He was probably sleeping. She didn't want to wake him.

On the other hand, if something was wrong, she needed to know. Why hadn't he at least sent her a text?

Tiffany grabbed the phone and carried it to the deck. She looked over the ocean. The moon cast a pleasant glow on it. A few people remained on the beach. Tiffany debated whether or not she should call her grandpa.

It could be that he was busy with a poker game. Sometimes those went pretty late. He and his friends took those games seriously. She was pretty sure that other things went down then too, but she never questioned it. Whenever they needed something, it was his poker buddies who came through.

That was how she got her car and new identity.

Tiffany looked up at the stars. Anxiety built in her chest. She needed to call. Otherwise, she wouldn't get any more sleep. Her stress levels would return to what they had been. He would understand a late-night call.

Once again, his number went to voice mail. She groaned, and then went back to the bed. Had he just forgotten his phone downstairs? If he was in his room, he would never hear it. It wasn't like him, but if he'd had a late night, maybe he did only forget it.

She tried a couple more times before giving up. Despite being worried, her eyelids became heavy again. If he was sleeping, she probably should too. If she didn't get rest, she wouldn't be able to drive the next morning. If her car was fixed the next day, she needed to get on the road. Even a few hours of driving would get her closer to wherever she was going.

He was probably fine—and would be upset with her for worrying. The simplest answer had to be the right one. But if that was the case, why wouldn't that nagging feeling leave her alone?

Tiffany turned off the TV and climbed under the covers. Surely, in the morning he would call. Maybe even really early, so that was all the more reason to get to sleep and stop letting her mind get the best of her.

She closed her eyes and pushed away every thought that came to mind. It was only a few minutes before she started to doze. Then the image of Jake's face showed up in her mind's eye: he smiled at her, and his tanned skin glistened in the warm sun. Tiffany sighed and rolled over, pulling the covers over her head.

The last thing she needed was a distraction like him—no matter how adorable he was. She couldn't trust a man, and she certainly didn't need one. Not after Trent. He had shown her that men couldn't be trusted, at least not with her heart. He had appeared to be kind and sweet at first, but he turned out to be a monster.

What she needed was to get far away from Trent and focus on getting a job and a place to live. Then she needed to find some friends—*girl* friends—and just enjoy the single life. She'd been too eager to get married and look how that turned out. Once she was busy with work and friends, she wouldn't have time to think about him anymore.

Jake had been a nice distraction the day before, but nothing else. She pushed his face out of her mind along with every other thought that had managed to enter.

First thing in the morning, she would go to the auto shop and find out the status of her car. Maybe the tattooed guy would have even spoken with her grandpa, and the car would already be in the process of being fixed.

Tiffany took a deep breath and held it as long as she could. She let it out slowly. It was time to stop thinking about everything that *could* be wrong and fall asleep thinking about what was *right* in her life.

She could fall asleep without worrying Trent would barge in and wake her, screaming about something stupid just to keep her from getting a good night's sleep. He didn't even know where she was.

The hotel was locked, keeping her safe. She could sleep as long as she wanted. Not only that, but she'd just had a relaxing day being pampered.

It gave her pleasure knowing how much that would have pissed Trent off, and even more since he couldn't do a thing about it.

Tiffany rubbed one of her nails, feeling the polish. Yes, she had made the right decision to leave home and start fresh. As she drifted off to sleep, Jake's handsome face smiled at her from her dreams.

Nine

~

JAKE PACED THE WAITING ROOM. "They said they would give us an update an hour ago. What's going on? I'm going to find out."

"Sit down, Son," said his mom. "They'll come out when they're ready. The good doctors are probably busy taking care of him."

"Or they forgot about us." Jake looked at the clock on the wall. "It's three in the morning. This is ridiculous."

His mom stared at him. Her tear-streaked face nearly broke him.

He sat next to her. "Do you really want to sit and wait? We need to remind them that we're here."

She dabbed her eyes with a tissue. "They know, Jake. And when they're ready, we'll be the first ones they talk to."

"I should take you home. You need some sleep. I'll leave a note for them to call the house with any news."

His mom patted his knee. "You should go home and

rest. I'll have them call you after they talk to me."

"Then what? How will you get home?"

"You can come back for me or I'm sure your brothers will be in town soon. They're all making preparations to fly in."

Jake made a face. "I can't leave you here alone."

His mom looked around the waiting room. "I'm hardly alone."

"What if you get hungry?"

"There's a cafeteria downstairs. I know where it is. Remember how often we ate there when—?"

"Yes. Dad isn't going to be here that long. He'll probably be home tomorrow, and ticked off that everyone flew in."

"True. All the more reason to go home. He'll want you manning the shop, not sitting here."

Jake shifted his weight in the seat. "I'll go home and rest—if you send one of my brothers to take over the shop tomorrow. There's no way I can be there all day after being here."

She leaned over and kissed his forehead. "I will. Get some rest and don't worry about me. I'll wait as long as it takes to see your dad."

He raised an eyebrow, holding a quick internal debate. "If you do need to come back home, don't hesitate to call. No matter the time."

"I'm fine."

"I hope so." Jake stood and then kissed the top of

her head. "I'll keep my cell on if you need me."

She nodded and then opened up her purse.

Jake stopped at the desk and let the nurse know that his mom was going to stay and he gave her his number. "Call me if she needs anything."

He watched his mom as he walked out of the waiting room. She appeared to be texting someone. At this hour, probably family. His brothers weren't the only ones on their way over. Aunts, uncles, and cousins were, too. It was going to be a family reunion minus the barbecue.

When he got off the elevator in the garage, he noticed a pay booth. He went up, paid his fees, and finally found his parents' car. He had to walk up and down several aisles before he found it, not knowing where his mom had parked. At least she'd been able to tell him which level.

Jake yawned as he started the car. It was about a half an hour drive home, so he decided to stop for coffee—if he could find anything open at that hour. If he would have thought about it, he could have gotten some before leaving the hospital. He wasn't going back now.

As he drove, he paid more attention to what was on the side of the road than the traffic around him.

A horn blared as he went through an intersection. He looked up to see a red light and waved an embarrassed apology.

No need to send himself to the hospital, also. He'd

give his mom a heart attack if both Jake and his dad there. Instead of looking for a coffee stand, he rolled down the window and turned up the radio. Talk radio screamed at him, and he changed it to his favorite station. He sang along with one of the popular songs from when he was in high school.

Before he knew it, he was back home. When he got inside, the answering machine—yes, his parents still insisted on one—flashed twelve new messages.

Jake threw his keys on the table. He didn't want to listen to them, and he sure wasn't calling anyone back. But what if the hospital or his mom had called? He'd told them both to call his cell, but he couldn't risk it. He grabbed a pad of paper and a pen, ready to take notes.

The messages played, and he wrote down who called. At least it would save his mom the trouble of listening to them. She could call everyone back from his notes. If she could read his chicken scratch. He could barely read it. Jake needed to get to sleep.

As the last message finished, he set the pen down and went to his room without bothering to get ready for bed. Even his shoes were still on. He threw himself on top of the covers and fell asleep, forgetting to set the alarm on his phone.

Ten

SUNLIGHT WOKE TIFFANY. SHE LOOKED at the alarm clock and saw that it was early. If she got going now, she could talk to the mechanic and then check out of the hotel if her car would be ready that day.

Her stomach rumbled, but she ignored it. Tiffany got ready as fast as she could, and then made her way to the auto shop. When she got there, her heart sank. The car still sat in the parking lot. Had he not even gotten to it yet?

Or could he possibly be done?

The tattooed guy from last time made eye contact with her as she walked in.

"Checking on your car?" he asked.

"Yeah. Is it ready?"

"We haven't been able to get it in yet. But we did manage to get it towed yesterday. You wouldn't believe how busy we've been."

"I can see that. Are you going to get to it this morning?" Tiffany looked around at all the other people waiting. She should have had it towed somewhere else, even if it would have been farther and more expensive.

He looked through some files and then motioned for Tiffany to come closer. "It looks like I won't get to until tomorrow."

Tiffany clenched her fists.

"But I can see you're not happy about that. If you do me a favor, I can move it up."

"What kind of favor?" She narrowed her eyes. What could he possibly want?

"I need something from the Hunter Family Shop. Do you know where that is? Over on Fourth and Rose."

Jake's shop. "I've been there." Her heart rate picked up.

"Tell him Bobby sent you." Bobby scribbled something on a scrap piece of paper and folded it several times. "Have him grab this for me. Once you bring it back, I'll move you up in priority."

Tiffany took the paper and tucked it into the outside pocket of her purse. "I don't suppose you've spoken with my grandfather?"

Bobby looked confused for a moment. "You wanted me to call him, right? If you wrote a note on the paperwork, I'll give him a call when the time comes. It'll be much faster if you can bring me the items written on the paper."

"I'll be back." Tiffany spun around and headed out the door. She pulled out her phone and saw no missed calls. Her stomach tightened. Something might have happened to her grandpa's phone and he couldn't get a hold of her. That had to be it. Trent was a jerk, but he wouldn't hurt Grandpa.

She would try again after she was done with her little mission. Jake's shop was a few blocks away, but the sidewalks were already getting crowded. Why would anyone be up so early on a vacation? She'd sleep in as late as possible if she were on a vacation. Tiffany looked around and noticed most of the people had kids or were older. She didn't really see anyone her age—probably because they were smart and sleeping.

Though it was crowded, she still made it to the shop in good time. She pushed on the door, but it wouldn't budge. She pushed again without success, and then looked inside. The lights were off and no one appeared to be inside.

Tiffany sighed. Now what? Was there somewhere else she could get what Bobby needed?

"Hey there, pretty lady."

She braced herself for a confrontation, but relaxed when she saw Dimitri. "Hi. Do you know where Jake is?"

"Looks like he stood up to his parents."

"What do you mean?"

"'Bout his long hours. Jake must be sleeping in. Strange that his parents would leave the shop closed, though. I'll see what I can find out. Want to help me?"

Tiffany shook her head. "I need to eat before I pass out. This morning hasn't been going the way I planned."

"Want me to text you when I find something out? What's your number?"

Her breath caught. She was keeping the number secret. Only her grandpa had it—wherever he was. "No thanks. I'll stop by after breakfast."

Dimitri gave her a curious look. "Okay. I promise to have some info for you when you return."

"Thanks." Tiffany turned around and walked back toward the auto shop. Her stomach growled as she looked for somewhere to eat. She was getting light-headed, so it wasn't time to be picky.

Tiffany found a deli and ordered a breakfast burrito. Another customer had one, and it looked huge. Perfect. She sat near the back when she finally got it. She had eaten the entire thing before she knew it.

She sat back, allowing her stomach to settle. Why couldn't things be easy? Or at least easier? It was good to be away from Trent—obviously. But she felt like a target, not being able to leave Kittle Falls.

Tiffany wasn't far enough away from home to stop and settle down. Sure, she was a couple states away, but barely. She hadn't driven too far after she crossed the California border before stopping in town.

The goal was to get to at least southern Cali before finding somewhere to settle. Maybe San Diego or something. Or possibly even going east. Texas was nice and big. It would be hard for Trent to find her. She'd never had any interest in going there, so it was somewhere Trent would never think to look.

"Are you done with the table?"

Tiffany looked up to see a family of five standing near her. All the other tables were full. "Yeah. You can have it." She picked up her trash and let them have the table. She tossed her stuff and went outside. It felt like it had heated up ten degrees since she had been inside.

Maybe Jake was back at the shop already. She made her way back and found that not only the shop was still closed, but Dimitri was nowhere in sight. Someone who looked like a younger version of Dimitri stood behind the newspaper stand.

She weaved her way through the crowds back to the auto shop and slammed Bobby's paper on the counter. "The shop is closed. A guy named Dimitri went on a quest to find out what's going on with Jake. I can't help you, so it looks like I'll just have to wait in line like everyone else. How long's it going to be?"

Bobby looked surprised. He raised the eyebrow that had a ring through it. "Don't be so hasty. I really need the things listed in there. We can still help each other out."

"How?" Tiffany crossed her arms. "And why me?"

"Hold on." Bobby pulled out a phone and scrolled his finger around the screen before putting it to his ear.

"Jake, you sound asleep. What are you doing?" He paused, his eyes widening. "Is everything all right?"

Tiffany's hear skipped a beat. Was Jake hurt worse than the gash in his side from the other evening?

"You going to open the shop today?" Bobby asked. "I've got a pretty girl here who wants to get over there. ... Right. ... Okay. Talk to you later, dude."

Tiffany's mouth felt dry. "Is everything okay?"

"He overslept."

She let out a sigh of relief.

"Were you worried?" He tilted his head as if trying to read her.

Tiffany shrugged. "He's a nice guy. I'd hate to see anything happen to him."

Bobby looked like he tried to restrain a smile. "He said he'd open the shop in about a half hour. If you can bring me that stuff, I can still move you up in the line."

"I hope he has Aspirin," Tiffany muttered. She picked the list back up and stormed out. What was she going to do for a half hour? She made her way to the street, heat rising from her core up to her head.

Tiffany felt like punching something. There was a street sign not far away. No, she'd only end up breaking her hand, and that was the last thing she needed. Not only that, but she'd be acting like Trent—and that was the last thing she wanted. She needed to take a few deep breaths and calm down.

People gathered around something across the street.

Maybe whatever it was would be enough to distract her until the shop opened and she could get whatever was so important to Bobby.

She crossed the road and saw a guy who had a monkey riding a tiny bike. Everyone circled around gasped and laughed at its tricks. Being in the mood she was in, Tiffany wasn't impressed, but she watched anyway. The monkey did a wheelie and the crowd broke into applause.

Tiffany looked at her phone. Twenty more minutes.

Eleven

~

JAKE GRABBED HIS PHONE BEFORE running out the door. His parents were going to chew him out for opening late. Even though he had told them he was going to work less, now that his dad was in the hospital, it was back to full days before he even had the chance to take a break.

He slammed the door shut and jiggled the knob to make sure it was locked. They never bothered with the other locks with crime being so low. As he ran to the shop, he couldn't help thinking of all the lost business. He hadn't looked at the time since Bobby called, but judging by how warm it was it had to be close to lunch.

When he got to the shop, Dimitri ran toward him shouting something.

"I gotta open the shop. I don't have time to talk." Jake pulled out the keys and unlocked the door. He flipped the open sign over before he was all the way inside, and then turned on the lights.

He ran his hands through his hair and looked

around. It was disorienting to start his day like this.

Dimitri came in. "Hey, I—"

"You buying something? Because I need to get things going." Jake sprinted to the till, and prepared it for a busy day.

"The beautiful girl came by looking for you this morning."

Jake froze. "Elena? She's still here? She came to the shop?"

"She said she'd be back. I thought you should know."

"Thanks." Jake ran his hands through his hair again. He'd only run a brush through it before he'd gotten dressed. He hadn't paid any attention to how he looked.

Dimitri walked to the counter. "Is everything okay? You don't look well."

"My dad is in the hospital. I was there most of the night, and then when I got home, I forgot to set my alarm. If Bobby hadn't called, I'd still be sleeping."

"What's wrong? Is he going to be fine?"

Jake rubbed his stubble. "I hope so. I don't know much yet. Some of my brothers are coming into town. They're probably taking care of Mom. I need to give someone a call to find out what's going on. I don't know why the hospital didn't call me. I left them my number."

"Like you said, your brothers are probably there. The staff probably figures they'll tell you what's going on."

"Doesn't give them an excuse. For all they know, I'm not on speaking terms with them."

"You're not?" Dimitri's eyes widened.

"Of course I am, but they don't know that."

"I'll give you some time to get the shop ready or call the hospital. I just wanted to let you know a pretty thing was looking for you. Tell your dad I hope he feels better."

Jake nodded. He picked up his phone, but before he could dial, customers rolled in. He slid the phone in his pocket and greeted the people as they walked by.

Tourists streamed in and out for the next ten minutes. Jake distracted himself with light conversation until there was a lull. He took advantage of it and called his mom.

"Hello, Jake." She sounded tired.

"Have you gotten any sleep?"

"Here and there. Brayden is here and he's talking with the nurses and doctors for me."

"Why don't you have him take you home? You need to rest."

"I'm waiting to see your dad."

"What?" Jake exclaimed. "You still haven't seen him?"

"Soon."

"Have they bothered to tell you what happened?"

"They think he had a stroke, or even a blood clot. They've been running a lot of tests since he isn't talking."

"Is he even awake?" Anger built in Jake's chest. "They can't keep you from him!"

"He woke up for a little while, but then passed out again."

"I need to get there."

"No, Jake. We need you manning the shop."

"Forget the shop. There are more important things—"

"No. We need the income. Now more than ever."

"You know what? My brothers are going to have to help me out. With everyone here, I'm not doing this on my own. Remember what I told you? Either I hire someone, or someone from the family needs to help. I can't keep these double shifts. Just wait, soon I'll be in the hospital before long."

"Don't talk like that."

"Why not? You and Dad have no right to put this kind of pressure on me. I need a break. I was the one who took care of—"

"Are you trying to get me admitted too? Don't talk to me like this."

Jake could hear Brayden talking in the background. After a moment, he spoke directly into the phone. "What's going on, Jake? Mom's here worried to pieces about Dad. Why are you adding to her stress?"

"I need to be there too, not stuck here in the shop."

"Well, someone needs to run it."

"Why is it always me? I'm sick of being treated like

the family baby."

"I need to be here to speak with the doctors. They can talk to me in ways they can't to Mom."

"Right." Jake kicked a pole. Brayden was a big-shot cardiologist in Dallas. "Is it Dad's heart? Is that the problem?"

If Brayden caught the sarcasm, he ignored it. "Doesn't appear so. They thought it might be a clot in the neck, but my money's on a stroke."

"You're betting on Dad's health now?"

"It's an expression. Don't you have customers to worry about?"

"Not at the moment. I heard there's some guy with a monkey on a bike near the beach, so all the tourists are there."

"Would you feel better if I called you as soon as I hear something?"

"Yeah. And if one of our brothers arrive, send them to help me out. I've been working double shifts this entire season."

"Ouch. I see why you're so grouchy. I'll call you when I know anything."

"I would appreciate it." Jake ended the call and put the phone on the counter.

The front door opened and he looked over. Elena walked in, and she was even more gorgeous than ever.

Jake held his breath and ran his fingers through his messy hair. And he probably looked horrible.

Twelve

~

TIFFANY PUSHED THE DOOR OPEN, surprised to find it moving after earlier. She had lost track of time watching the dumb monkey, and now she was thirsty after standing in the sun for so long. The door closed behind her.

She looked at the counter to find Jake already looking at her. His hair was pointing in several directions, and his nine o'clock shadow was turning into a full beard. He looked like he had just rolled out of bed, which according to Bobby was what had happened.

He looked adorable.

The last thing she wanted was to think that, but she couldn't help it. He was so cute, and looked snuggly. Part of her wanted to go behind the counter and wrap her arms around him.

They stared at each other, but it wasn't awkward.

"So, uh, you overslept?" Tiffany asked, the corners of her mouth curving upward. She walked toward the counter, forcing her legs to move slower than they wanted. She didn't want to appear too eager...or admit how excited she was to see him. All of her senses felt more alive than they had in a long time.

Jake ran his fingers over his beard, and then through his messy hair. "You could say that." He looked a little insecure, and Tiffany had the sudden urge to hold him and melt in his embrace. It was too bad they weren't in the hotel lobby where they could sneak off to a fireplace and sit in front of it.

Tiffany examined his features. There were dark circles under his eyes, and the creases on his forehead were more prominent than before. "Did you get any sleep?" she asked, concerned.

His face softened. "Not much. My dad went to the hospital last night, and I was there with my mom until early this morning."

Her eyes widened. "Oh, no. Is he okay?"

Jake frowned. "We don't really know anything yet. Even so, the shop must go on." He sighed, looking exhausted.

"You must be so worried." She cringed. What a stupid thing to say. Of course he would be worried.

"I am. It's nice to see you, though. What a wonderful surprise." Jake looked like he meant it. "How much longer are you staying in town?"

Tiffany shrugged. "Until my car is ready, although at the current speed, I could be here all year."

Jake's eyes lit up, but then his face returned to

sleepy. Or was that disappointment? "Yeah, Bobby stays busy. You probably can't wait to get out of here."

That reminded Tiffany of why she came to the store. She pulled out Bobby's list and handed it to Jake. "Speaking of Bobby, he said he needs whatever's on the list." Suddenly she wasn't so eager to leave, but she knew she couldn't let herself fall for anyone right now. No matter how wonderful and sweet Jake was. Tiffany didn't want to rebound, and Jake certainly didn't deserve that.

He took the list, but didn't unfold the paper. His gaze remained on her. "How far back is he backlogged?"

Tiffany shrugged again. "He said he'd move me up in the line if I get him what's on that list. With any luck, I could leave tonight." But the thought didn't make her feel so lucky.

Jake's face fell. Or was that her imagination? "Well, if you're stuck here for a while, maybe we can hang out again." He definitely looked hopeful. Could he feel the same way that she did? His brown eyes were full of intensity as he stared into hers. "I had a really good time with you the other night, Elena."

Elena. Would she ever get used to being called that? Shivers ran through her as she realized she could get used to anything he called her. She fought to find her voice. "I had fun, too. Tell you what. If you find whatever's on the list, I'll come back and help you with the shop until my car's ready."

"Really? You'd do that?"

"Yeah. You look like you could use the help. I could even grab some coffee on my way back. I get the feeling you could use that, also."

"I could." He unfolded the paper, and then raised an eyebrow. "You said this is what Bobby needed?" He looked befuddled, and it was adorable.

Tiffany pulled some hair behind her ear. "Whatever's on that list is my golden ticket to get out of here."

"If you say so. I'll grab them for you." He went to the back of the store, and came back carrying three tree-shaped air fresheners.

Tiffany looked back and forth between Jake and the scented trees. "What are those for?"

"It's what Bobby wants."

"*That* was what he needed so badly?" Tiffany asked, scratching her head. Was Bobby messing with her?

"Wanna see the list?" Jake held it up.

"Show me." It didn't make any sense. Why would a mechanic send her on a goose chase after air fresheners? He had to have sold them himself.

Jake held the list up for her to see. Sure enough, the three different scented trees were written out. "Did he give you any money for these?"

Tiffany frowned. "No. Looks like I'll have to pay for them." She opened her purse.

"Don't worry about it."

"I'm the one who wants my car fixed faster. It's my

payment."

"You're getting me coffee, right?" Jake asked. "We'll call it even."

"Are you sure? I can buy them."

Jake yawned. "It's on the house. Or if you'd feel better, consider an exchange for the coffee. I'm in the mood for an iced mocha." He grinned.

Tiffany again wanted to snuggle up to him. She cleared her throat instead. "Okay. I'll be back." She grabbed the trees from Jake, and hurried outside before she found herself actually cuddling up against him. Tiffany had only met him the other day. How could she be so attracted to him already?

It could be a rebound—she'd done that before in her teen years. But in those days, she had been running from a broken heart, not wanting to give herself time to heal.

This, she had to admit was different. Yes, she was broken, but not because of her heart. She had left Trent emotionally long before she took off physically. Tiffany hadn't been in love since she was a newlywed.

Jake made her feel emotions she'd locked and buried long ago. Tiffany never thought she would be able to trust or love again, and though she wasn't ready to make the jump, Jake gave her hope that someday she could. No matter how kind and gentle he appeared, she had to be careful because looks could be deceptive.

Dimitri called to her, pulling her out of her

thoughts. The last thing she wanted was to talk to anyone. Tiffany needed to make sense of everything.

"Can't talk. Sorry." She moved away from the building, picked up her speed, going in the opposite direction of Dimitri. Looking at the air fresheners made heat rise through her body. Why had Bobby sent her to get those? Was he toying with her?

Tiffany knew the irritation was from thinking about Trent. He put her in a bad mood whether he was present or not. Angry tears welled in her eyes. Why hadn't she left him sooner? Before things had gotten to the point where she needed a new identity and new location which forced her to leave her grandpa?

When she got to the auto shop, she had to wait behind a lady who asked about five hundred questions. Tiffany's irritation only grew. When the annoying woman in front of her was finally satisfied, Tiffany threw the trees on Bobby's desk. "Here you go." She wanted to throw them at *him*, but smiled sweetly instead. More tears threatened, but she wouldn't give in. "Happy? You must have really needed them."

Bobby laughed, only angering her further. "Sure did. My back room is getting smelly, and these are my favorite scents. I'm out of stock."

"Right. So, when are you going to finally look at my car?"

He picked up a stack of papers and flipped through them. "All the spots are full now, but as soon as one opens up, I'll bring in yours. Pinky promise." Bobby held up a pinky.

Tiffany ignored it. "How long?"

"Depends. Could be five minutes or two hours. It just depends on how fast we can fix the ones ahead of you."

Tiffany leaned against the counter, pressing her hands down. "That's not helpful."

"Sorry." He didn't look sorry.

"Don't forget to call my grandpa. He wants to talk to you before you touch it. He's the one paying the bill."

"No problem. We'll figure out what's wrong and then give him a shout. Anything else?"

"It would be nice if you could let me know what's going on, too. Not just him."

"Will do. Oh, hey, I have a question for Jake. Would you mind asking him if—?"

Anger flared in her chest. "What is this? The dark ages? Call him yourself. He's exhausted from being at the hospital all night, and I need to bring him coffee. Tell me, is that stand across the street the only one around here?"

"There's a couple others, but that's the closest. Why was Jake at the hospital? Is he okay?"

"He's fine. Not sure about his dad, though."

"Oh crap. What happened?"

"I don't know anything. You're calling him anyway,

remember?"

"Okay, okay. One more thing."

Tiffany's shoulders dropped. "What?"

"He likes mint mochas."

Her anger melted away. "How do you know?" And why was he telling her?

Bobby leaned back in the chair. "Went to school with his older brother, Cruz. Jake helped me out with some stuff back in the day, and I couldn't pay him back. So he had me make him mint mochas when I worked at the coffee stand. He could never get enough of those."

That made sense. He had picked out chocolate chip mint ice cream the other night. "Why tell me?" Tiffany asked.

"I feel like I still owe him. Also, he's a good guy." Bobby stared into her eyes. He seemed to be trying to tell her that she needed to take care of him. Were her feelings for Jake that obvious?

Tiffany backed up. "Okay. Thanks for the tip." She went outside and headed for the coffee stand, her emotions swirling. She ordered an iced mint mocha for Jake and a latte with a double shot for her. She needed the extra caffeine.

Tiffany sipped her drink and looked across the street. Her car still sat in the parking lot. She found herself relieved for the excuse to stick around Kittle Falls longer.

Thirteen

JAKE GRABBED CHANGE FROM THE till and handed it to the frazzled-looking customer. She shoved it in her purse as her three kids dragged her to the door. Jake called out a thanks and turned to the next customer.

The shop phone rang. He picked it up. "Hunter Family Store. Jake speaking."

"Jake, man. Is your dad okay?" It was Bobby.

"I don't know. Brayden's over there using his doctor-speak. Nobody thinks I need to be kept informed." He scanned the customer's items. "Hold on, Bobby." He set the phone down and finished the transaction, and then picked the phone back up. "What was the deal with the air fresheners?"

"Hey dude, I needed them. It was an emergency. When you need them, it can't wait." Jake could almost hear Bobby smiling.

"Thanks for sending her my way."

"Are you two going to spend some time together?" Bobby sounded almost as eager for it as Jake.

"Yeah. Elena offered to bring me coffee." Jake tried to keep his voice steady, but there was no hiding his true feelings from a friend as good as Bobby.

"Want me to stall on her car? You know I will."

Jake's heart skipped a beat. He sure did want Bobby to wait on the car, but then he remembered to look on Elena's face when she talked about leaving town. "That's not right. She wants—"

"I didn't ask that, Jake. You know I still owe you. What do you *want*?"

Jake imagined Elena's long, beautiful hair and bright green eyes. "I want to get to know her more."

"There's my answer. I'll send Randy here to the desk and I'll take care of her car personally."

"Be nice." Jake hoped Bobby wouldn't cause more damage to Elena's car.

"You know I will, bro. I'll take my sweet time, too. Look over the whole car. Check everything out in slow, pain-staking detail. We have to be sure not to miss anything that could be wrong with it."

"Thanks, Bobby." Despite the guild stabbing at him, excitement rose from his core. He would get to spend more time with Elena. Maybe, just maybe, he could even convince her to stay a little longer. Maybe even a lot longer.

"Tell me how it goes."

"I will. Thanks again."

"Not necessary." The call ended, and Jake put the

phone on the receiver. He was so out of practice with the dating thing that he would probably screw it up, but at least he had a chance. There was something different about Elena. She wasn't like all the other girls who came through town.

His eyelids grew heavy, so he walked around to the front of the counter and adjusted the candy in some of the displays. He moved to the other side of the counter and rearranged some plastic kiddie sunglasses that were all out of order. If he kept moving around, he would stay awake until the next customer needed help...or until Elena arrived.

Jake glanced over at the door and saw Elena standing outside. She was watching him.

Heat crept into his cheeks. His pulse raced, causing his entire body to heat up for reasons other than the heat outside.

Elena held up one white cup with a brown sleeve and one clear cup with ice and brown liquid. He rushed to the door and held it open for her, hoping she wouldn't notice his flushed skin.

"Thank you. Here's a mocha for you." She held one of the cups for him. If she noticed anything was amiss, she didn't let on.

Before taking it, he asked, "Do you want me to pay you back? I—"

"No. Just enjoy the drink." Elena smiled, looking eager for him to take it. She pushed it closer to him.

"Okay. Thanks." He took the cup and sipped his mocha. Sweet mint flavoring filled his taste buds along with the chocolate. "Mint?"

Elena smiled, looking shy. "I heard you like it."

"I do. Thank you." He took another sip, allowing the caffeine to make its way into his bloodstream while the mint lingered in his mouth. "It's my favorite. I haven't had one in a long time."

"No?"

"I've been too busy to worry about treating myself to things like that."

She took a sip of hers, and then smiled sweetly at him. Jake's stomach twisted in a knot. She was gorgeous, but not in a way where she seemed to know it like so many other women.

"Want me to show you around the shop while it's quiet? It's sure to fill up any minute."

"Nah. I explored the other day. Remember?"

He sure did. It was the first time he'd laid eyes on her. She had been so sad, but in the short time since then, she had grown happier. "Want to have a seat instead?" he asked. "We have a couple chairs behind the register. I usually stand, but you look like you could use a break—not that you look bad." Ugh. Why did he always have to get his foot stuck in his mouth? That was part of the reason girls who liked him always wanted one of his brothers instead.

Elena didn't seem to notice Jake's poor choice of

words. "Sure." She took a sip, and walked toward the counter.

He stood back, watching her. Every move she made melted his insides. He hadn't thought he wanted a relationship, but she changed everything. His family may be a wreck, and he was a mess, but she made him want to pull himself together and become the best version of himself.

His sister's face showed up in his mind's eye. "Go on, Jake. Win the girl," Sophia seemed to say to him.

Jake stopped in his tracks.

"Move on, sweet brother. Don't let me hold you back. I know how much you miss me, but I want you to find happiness. Live your life, and enjoy it." Her image dissolved.

"Wait," he whispered to Sophia.

Elena turned around. "What?"

Jake shook his head. "Nothing. Just enjoying my mocha." He took another sip, and then caught up with her.

She put her cup on the counter and looked at the disorganization he called his work station. "You know what this place needs?"

"A bull dozer?" Jake joked.

Her eyes sparkled. "It's not that bad. You'd feel a lot better if all this had some order. Mind if I help?"

"I won't stop you. I'd offer to help, but I'd probably get in your way."

"Don't even think about it. I'm here to help. You can sit and doze if you want."

"That would be rude."

"Get some sleep. I got this." Elena moved some things around on the counter.

Jake sat in one of the chairs and watched as she pulled things from the shelves and spread everything around the floor behind the counter. Just when the ground was covered, the door dinged announcing a new wave of customers.

Elena turned to him. "I have this too." She turned to the customers and welcomed them. Then she picked up a stack of papers from the floor and moved them on top of another stack.

More people came in, and she called out hellos to each one. When a young couple came to the counter, Jake stood.

Elena shook her head. "I said I got this. Relax."

"You can do the till?" he asked.

"I worked retail in high school." She turned to the customers and rang them up twice as fast as Jake ever had, even on his best day.

What a woman. He ran his hand along his jawline as he watched as Elena. She got through the line in record time, each person leaving with a smile on their face.

After the store the store emptied, she sat down next to him. "Is it always busy like that?"

"This time of year it is. You were unbelievable." In

more ways than one. He couldn't believe how amazing she was: kind, generous, thoughtful, a hard worker, and more beautiful than anyone he had ever dreamed of giving him any attention.

Pink covered her face from his compliment. "I was rusty at first, but then everything came back to me. It was nothing, really."

"Don't say that. You're amazing."

Her face grew darker. They stared at each other, the intensity building. Before either could say anything, more customers came in.

By the time the shop emptied again, Jake could barely keep his eyes open, even with as much as he enjoyed watching Elena.

She sat next to him. "I can't believe you do this every day."

Jake tried to stifle a yawn. "I should pay you. I feel like I'm taking advantage of you."

"Nonsense." Elena shook her head. "Seriously, I'm just glad to have something to do."

He yawned, unable to keep that one in.

She pushed his shoulder playfully. "Besides, you obviously need some rest. I'm glad to help you out. Do you want to go back home and get some more sleep?"

Jake's eyelids were growing heavier by the minute. "No. I can't do that to you."

"Why not? I've got everything under control here. You were up all night, and will probably be again tonight."

She made sense, but his parents would kill him for leaving the store…if they found out. What was Elena going to do? Rob them? She had nowhere to go, and her car was in Bobby's shop. Also, if he was manning the place himself, he would probably fall asleep, and then someone actually would rob them.

He stretched and then stood up. "You drive a tough bargain."

A smile spread wide across her face. She was so dang beautiful. He would almost rather spend the time watching her work than going back home to sleep. If he could stay awake. Not even the iced mint mocha helped.

"Go on," she said. "I'll have this place organized and full of happy customers when you get back."

"I'm sure you will. I'll be back before closing. This time I'll set my alarm."

"You'd better." She smiled again. "Can I get your number just in case?" She pulled out her cell phone.

He told her his number and she put it in her phone.

She stood. "Now get some sleep. I've got this."

"Thanks, Elena. I really appreciate it."

"This is actually kind of fun. Go."

"I'm leaving. Sheesh. Can't believe I'm getting kicked out of my own shop."

She gave him another playful shove and their eyes met, holding the gaze. Jake held his breath. He couldn't stop looking at those gorgeous green eyes. Never before had he seen a color like that.

The front door bell rang, announcing the next rush of customers.

"Go on," she whispered.

He nodded, unable to find his voice. Jake made his way outside, unable to think of anything other than Elena and her bright green eyes.

"Leaving so soon?"

Jake turned to see Dimitri near his stand. Jake cleared his throat, finally able to speak. "Yeah. I'm going to get some more rest. Elena's taking care of the store. Can you keep an eye on her, just in case she needs help? She's doing really well, but I don't want her getting overwhelmed."

"Then why leave?"

"I'm beat, and she insisted."

"Sure, I'll check in on her."

"Thanks. I appreciate it." He yawned again.

"Get out of here, Jake." Dimitri laughed. "You obviously need sleep."

Fourteen

THE LAST CUSTOMER LEFT, AND Tiffany finally sat down. Her feet ached, but it felt good to have been distracted for a while. She looked at the area behind the register and smiled. She'd at least made a difference. It had been so disorganized, but now everything had its place, and it looked good, too.

She had even moved around some of the displays in front of the counter, and she had already seen results. People had bought more of those items afterward. Not only that, it was nice to be needed for a change.

The door dinged, and she jumped to her feet, ready to greet the next customer. But it wasn't a patron.

Jake walked in. He had his hair slicked back, un-wrinkled clothes, and a freshly shaved face. Tiffany's breath caught. He looked like he could have been in one of the magazines on the rack he just passed. Actually, he looked better than those stuffy models. She had the overwhelming desire to run her fingers over his smooth face.

"Did you do all this? It looks wonderful." He looked at the front of the counter.

Tiffany struggled to find her voice. She could stare at him all day. "I just moved some things around." It was nothing compared to the way he looked.

"No, really. It looks so professional. Much better than before. I can't believe it."

"Oh, stop." Tiffany looked away, embarrassed.

Jake moved to where she looked, and stared into her eyes. "I love it. Will you let me take you out to dinner?"

Tiffany's heart raced. "Don't you have to get to the hospital? What about your dad?"

Jake shook his head. "Two of my brothers are there with my parents, and they say he's doing a lot better. I can go later since I just slept. Will you join me for a meal?"

She nodded, suddenly feeling shy. He was the only person who made her feel that way. "Can I go back to my hotel room and freshen up? I've been working all day." The corners of her mouth curved upward.

"No problem. I'll close up here, and then pick you up at the hotel in an hour?" His eyes held an eagerness that made her heart jump into her throat.

Tiffany cleared her throat. "That's perfect. See you then." She hurried to the door before she gave into the increasing desire to jump into his arms. She wanted to wrap her arms around him and take in his freshly-showered smell. She gave a little wave as she went through the door, hoping he didn't notice what he did to her.

Tiffany made sure to walk past the auto shop on her way to the hotel. Her car was still in the parking lot. Did that mean it hadn't moved? Or had it been fixed? She *had* gotten those super-important air fresheners for Bobby.

She went inside, finding Bobby sweeping. "Did you get to my car?" *Please say no.*

Bobby looked up. "Sorry, Sweets. All the cars ahead of you today had serious problems. I'm not even sure I'll get to yours tomorrow."

Tiffany bit her lower lip, pretending to think about it. Then she shrugged. "Well, don't forget to call my grandpa before you do anything." She spun around and went back to her hotel.

When she got to her room, she looked around. What was she going to wear? She only had the one suitcase, and she hadn't packed for a date. It didn't matter. She would make it work. With a spring in her step, she made her way to the bed, dumping her entire 'wardrobe' onto it. Tiffany finally settled on a cute lacy top that she could wear over a camisole and skinny jeans. The lace top was a little wrinkled, but if she hung it in the bathroom while she showered, it should lose the wrinkles.

When she was done getting ready, she noticed a light blinking on her phone. Had she missed a call? She ran to her bed and picked it up. She had a new text from Grandpa.

Some stuff came up with a friend. Sorry I haven't returned your calls. Have fun, and let me know what's going on.

Relief washed over her. He was okay, just busy. She looked at the time, and decided to call him back later. Jake was supposed to meet her any minute.

Tiffany went down to the lobby and saw him standing by the doors. He was looking at the elevators, but she had come down the staircase. He looked her way just as she went down the final few steps.

Jake broke into a wide smile, and then walked toward her. He wore slacks and a dress shirt, and he looked even better than before. Tiffany's heart raced, and she gave him a nervous smile. Her body temperature rose, and the smell of her citrus perfume surrounded her from the heat.

"You look stunning." He pulled a bright bouquet of flowers from behind his back.

She let out a small gasp. "Are those for me?"

Jake smiled wider. "Who else?"

Her face heated even more. Tiffany didn't know how to take a compliment, but she would find a way. "Thank you. They're beautiful."

"They're nothing compared to you." He pushed them closer to her.

She reached for the flowers, and her fingers brushed against his. Chills ran down her back, and not from the hotel's air conditioning.

"Can I get a picture?" he asked.

"Of me?" Her stomach dropped to the floor. Did she dare leave photographic evidence of being in Kittle Falls?

Jake looked at her with curiosity. "Why does it surprise you?"

She looked down and shrugged. How could she explain? Would she make it through the date, or would he figure out that she was broken and run for the hills? As much as she wanted to be Elena, she was still Tiffany. There was no erasing her past, and that was the last thing she wanted to explain to him.

"Can I get a picture of us?" he asked. "Please. You look so pretty holding the flowers."

Tiffany looked back up and held his gaze. His beautiful, kind brown eyes pleaded with her. Jake was so sweet that she didn't want to let him down. He was trustworthy—her heart told her that much. She was going to change her appearance when she got to her new home anyway, so it probably wouldn't do any harm to have a picture with him.

It would be nice to have a picture of the memory, also. She didn't want to forget him, and she could imagine herself looking at the image of them with fondness years later when she was old and gray.

She nodded an okay, and then his face lit up. Her heart fluttered, and she knew she had made the right decision. He grabbed the attention of someone walking by, and then asked her to take a picture.

Before Tiffany knew what was going on, she stood next to Jake in front of a potted palm tree. He put his arm around her, seeming nervous. She felt safe, and nestled a little closer.

The lady took a few pictures with Jake's cell phone, and then handed it back to him, smiling. "You two are so cute."

"Thanks." Jake took his phone and scrolled through the images, showing the picture to Tiffany. It was strange seeing a picture of her with someone other than Trent, but she liked it. Unable to keep from smiling, she realized the lady was right. She and Jake did look good together.

"Can you send those to me?" she asked.

"I could…but you'd have to give me your number." Jake had a curious look.

Butterflies danced in her stomach. She hadn't given it to anyone, but she realized she wanted Jake to have it. She pulled out her phone, nearly dropping it, and then called him.

A Rod Stewart song came from his phone. He turned it off fast, his face turning pink. "That was my sister's favorite song. It's in memory of her. I swear."

Tiffany held back a smile. "You don't have to explain anything to me."

"I didn't want you thinking that's what I listen to in my free time."

"Do you even have any free time?" she asked.

He shook his head. "I wouldn't recognize a single song released in the last two years."

"Me, neither." Unless it was country. That was all Trent would allow when he was around. He had even stocked songs in her car to listen to when she drove. "So, where are we going?"

"Somewhere I love, but never go enough. It's about twenty minutes away. Is that okay?"

"I don't have any other plans." Tiffany slid her phone back into her purse.

"Good." He held out his hand.

Tiffany's pulse pounded in her ears. Holding his hand didn't seem like much, but it felt enormous.

Jake looked at her expectantly. "Are you ready?"

She took his hand and smiled, ignoring her nerves. Nothing better than pushing aside everything Trent had told her over the years to help her move away from him. "I can't wait." She meant it.

Jake led her to the parking lot. They went to a brown car that looked about twenty years old. "Sorry about the car," he said. "It belongs to my parents. I really need one of my own."

"It's fine. How's your dad?"

"He's sleeping a lot, but everyone keeps saying how

fast he's improving." He let go of her hand and unlocked the passenger side door with the key.

"Do they know what happened?"

"They thought a stroke at first, but now that he's doing so well, they're looking into other options. They'll have to take another MRI tomorrow."

"That sounds like good news. I hope I get to meet him when he gets out." Tiffany's eyes widened. She hadn't meant to say that, but it came out so naturally.

Jake looked as surprised as she felt. "I'd like that." He held the door open for her.

She sat, and he closed the door for her.

Tiffany felt like a princess.

Fifteen

JAKE WALKED AROUND THE BACK of the car, shaking his head. How could Elena have made herself even prettier than before? He couldn't believe that she actually wanted to spend time with him. It was time to get a haircut or something. He just didn't measure up.

She was the gorgeous, mysterious out-of-towner, and he was just the local boy running a tiny, outdated shop. He had barely left Kittle Falls his whole life. Elena would surely leave as soon as Bobby fixed her car. What did he or the town have to offer that someone like her? Elena was probably on her way somewhere exciting. That had to be why she didn't want to talk about it— she didn't want to make him feel bad.

He sat in the driver's seat and took a deep breath. The car smelled of the flowers and Elena's perfume. It was perfect, and he wanted to hold onto the scent for as long as he could.

She smiled at him, still holding the flowers.

Jake wanted to take another picture. He would need

as many as possible so he wouldn't forget a thing about her. None of his brothers would believe he had managed to catch the attention of someone so beautiful.

He started the car and looked forward. He needed to focus on driving, or they would never get to the restaurant. "Want some music?"

"As long as it's Rod Stewart." She grinned.

Jake laughed. She had a sense of humor, too. Was she perfect? It was starting to look that way. He turned on the radio, and Barry Manilow blasted from the speakers. He turned the volume down. "I swear, that's my mom's station. And she's deaf. Really, really deaf." How had the station gotten turned, anyway? Had one of his brothers driven his mom while Jake worked?

Elena laughed. "So, you're not only a closet Rod Stewart fan, but Barry Manilow too?"

Jake faked a guilty expression. "Now you know. Sure you wanna go out with me? There's still time to back out." Though he joked, part of him feared that she would take him up on the offer.

She put her hand up to her chin and pretended to think about it. "I'll take my chances."

Relief swept through him. "Glad to hear it." He pulled out of the parking spot before she could change her mind.

They made small talk on the way to the restaurant. As it turned out, Elena had graduated high school the year after him, so they mostly talked about high school days, comparing favorite bands and movies. At least they had similar tastes. Jake hoped that would help her forget about Barry Manilow.

When he pulled into the restaurant parking lot, he was glad to find it was relatively empty. You never knew during tourist season. If it had been a Friday or Saturday night, they would have been lucky to find a spot without a doubt.

Elena started to open her door.

"Hold it. Let me get that." Jake hurried around the car and opened the door for her.

"Thank you." She got out, and he closed it, locking it manually.

Jake took her hand, and they walked to the front doors. Teenagers ran by, yelling and teasing each other. When they got inside, he gave them his name. Elena went into the bathroom, and he took a seat. A couple across from them were all over each other. Jake looked away, wanting to tell them to get a room. He was going to have a hard enough time impressing Elena without those guys making conversation awkward. Kids ran around, bumping into people. Hopefully they would all be seated before Elena came out.

He looked over at the couple seated next to them. The man spoke about his day at work, oblivious that the lady next to him clearly had no interest. In fact, she looked like she wanted to be anywhere else.

Jake shook his head. What an atmosphere. Had he

chosen the wrong restaurant, or the wrong night? With any luck, everything at the table would be better. He had wanted a nice night to hopefully convince Elena to stay longer.

Obviously, they weren't at the point where they could start a relationship. The day they'd met, Jake hadn't thought he was ready for one, period. But somehow she'd already changed his mind. He wanted to get to know her and find out if it was at least a possibility for her, despite the fact she was so eager to get out of town.

The two annoying couples were taken to tables, and Elena was still in the restroom. Jake eyed the bathroom door. If she took much longer, he would ask someone to check on her. What if she got scared and took off? No, she wouldn't do that. It was too far to walk back to the hotel. Unless she had decided to take a cab. What if she asked someone leaving to give her a ride back?

"I've got to pull myself together," he muttered. He leaned back, took a deep breath, and watched the others around him. They didn't help to ease his frayed nerves.

At long last, Elena came out of the bathroom. Her hair was pulled back away from her face, but it still fell over her back behind her shoulders. She looked like an angel.

She sat next to him. "Sorry it took me so long in there. My hair didn't look right, so I fixed it. Well, I tried but all I did was make it worse, so I had to fix *that*.

It probably doesn't look any better than it did before...." She grabbed a strand and twirled it. "Sorry."

"You look fantastic. But you didn't need to change anything."

Elena looked away, and then turned back to him. "This place is busy for a weekday."

Why the change of subject? She seemed so uncomfortable whenever he gave her compliments. When he gave her the flowers and asked to take her picture, she squirmed like he had asked her to do something crazy. Jake gave her a smile he hoped would reassure her that he was normal. "Yeah, but you should see it here on the weekends. You have to wait outside before coming in here to wait."

"Hunter," called a server.

"That's us." Jake stood and took her hand. He loved the way her soft skin felt against his. She hadn't yet protested holding his hand, so he was going to as much as she'd let him. There was something different about her that made every little thing exciting, even just hand-holding.

When they got to the table, Elena's eyes widened and her hands covered her mouth. They were by a window that looked out over the Pacific Ocean. "It's beautiful."

"I'm glad you like it," Jake said. "I asked specifically for a view."

"I love it." When they settled in, she looked up from

the menu. "What should I get?"

"Everything's delicious. You can't go wrong." He opened up his, although he already knew what he wanted.

Elena squirmed in her seat before turning back to the menu.

"Is everything okay?" Jake asked. She looked really uncomfortable. "Do you want to go somewhere else?"

"No, no. I can't decide. I just thought you might have a suggestion." Elena looked like she would break into a sweat.

Jake sat taller and spoke in a soft tone, hoping to help her feel at ease. "I'm going to have the salmon pasta on page seven. I was stuck between that and the lobster one."

"Lobster sounds good—if that's okay. Or are we going dutch? I didn't even think to ask." She squirmed some more. "Sorry." A pained expression covered her face.

"I invited you, so it's my treat. Don't even look at the prices, okay?"

She looked confused, and then relieved. "Okay. I…I'm not really used to ordering for myself."

Jake wanted to ask why, but thought she would have a nervous breakdown if he did. Pretending to look at his menu, he studied her as she scanned the pages. Elena was adorable when flustered, but at the same time, she appeared defeated. He felt bad for her. Why would ordering dinner be so hard?

It was then he realized just how little he actually knew about her. Clearly, if he wanted her to let him in, he was going to have to be gentle. She had obviously been through something difficult if simple things like receiving flowers, taking pictures, and choosing food caused her such grief. Jake's heart ached, thinking about what—or probably who—could have done that to her.

Back at the shop, she had been so confident and happy. It was like she had been a completely different person. Jake thought the way she acted earlier must have been her letting go of whatever bothered her now.

Jake wanted to be the one to help her break free of her past—whatever it was.

Elena set down the menu, and then looked out the window at the water.

"Did you decide?" asked Jake.

"Yeah. Are you sure I can order anything?"

"Anything." He smiled, hoping to reassure her. "Thanks for all your help with the shop today. You were a lifesaver—and the counter looks great. I can't remember the last time everything was so nice."

Sixteen

~

TIFFANY PUSHED THE DISH AWAY. She'd eaten too much, but didn't care. The food had been delicious, and she'd actually been allowed to order her own meal for a change. Not only that, but Jake seemed genuinely interested in her, paying her compliments.

"Are you in the mood for dessert?" he asked.

She grasped her stomach and shook her head. "I don't have any room."

"Me, neither, but somehow I can always make room for ice cream." He raised his eyebrows, looking adorable, and obviously trying to change her mind.

"Go for it. I'll watch you eat." She smiled, feeling more at ease than she had before the meal.

He pouted. "That's no fun."

She laughed. "You're pretty convincing, but I would explode right here. You don't want to see that."

Jake pretended to think about it. "You're right. It would make a huge mess. The staff might make me stay to clean it up."

Tiffany shook her head, holding back a laugh. "See? I couldn't do that to you."

"Well, since you don't want dessert, are you up for a walk by the water? There's a path behind the building that goes down there." He pointed out the window.

She looked down at the empty beach. "That would be fun. I need to walk off this dinner, anyway." She groaned. Why had she eaten so much on a date? And why had she said that? "I mean, I'd love to walk down there with you. Sorry, I'm not used to this dating thing."

"Do I make you nervous?" His eyes showed concern.

"No. You're sweet and funny." And charming…and handsome.

"What is it, then?" He rested his chin on his palm, looking into her eyes.

Butterflies danced in her stomach. "I just haven't been on a date in a long time."

"Well, I'm honored you said yes. Truth be told, I haven't been on one in ages, either."

"You haven't?" Tiffany couldn't keep the surprise out of her voice. As attractive as he was, she would've thought he'd take a new girl out every week as the tourists rotated in and out of town.

The waiter arrived with the check, and Jake handed him a credit card. He turned back to Tiffany. "I haven't. You walked into the shop at the most unexpected time. The last thing I was thinking about was going on a date, but spending time with you is exactly what I needed."

"Really?" Her heartbeat pounded in her ears.

He nodded.

"You kind of had the same effect on me," Tiffany whispered, her nerves calming. He looked so reassuring. They stared into each other's eyes. She realized she didn't feel nervous anymore. As Tiffany stared into his deep brown eyes, she felt she was with someone trustworthy.

That was huge.

Before she knew it, they were walking down a dirt path behind the restaurant, hand in hand. She was hyper-aware of his hand, and couldn't help focusing on each movement. She didn't want to hold too tight or too loose, and she didn't want to squeeze or sweat. There was so much to think about, and it was just a simple thing.

They got down to the water's edge, and the beach was just as empty as it had been when they looked out from the restaurant.

"It's beautiful down here. I can't believe it's not crowded."

"It's one of the places tourists don't know about. The locals are usually busy working all summer, but you should see it when school starts."

"Why?"

"Everyone gathers for bonfires. The beach is filled with Frisbee and volleyball. It's a lot of fun—a great time to unwind after a busy summer."

"Sounds like a good time, but I'm glad we're here now. It's nice to have it to ourselves." Tiffany squeezed his hand, and then after realizing that she had, she held her breath.

He squeezed back, still looking out at the water. He took Tiffany's other hand and rubbed his thumb over her palm. Her skin tingled along the path he followed. She watched his thumb until he stopped, and then she looked up to his face.

They made eye contact. Tiffany opened her mouth to speak, but no words came. Her mind raced, and a rush of feelings ran through her. She wanted to kiss him, or rather for him to kiss her. But at the same time, she feared it. Everything was happening so fast. She wanted to give in, but she also feared what would happen after that?

Would she fall in love? Or would she only set herself up for more heartache?

Tiffany looked into his eyes, wanting to know his thoughts. Did he want to kiss her? Was he waiting for her to give a sign of approval?

He let go of her hand, and pulled some hair behind her ear, his finger lingering against it.

"Want to follow the path?" he asked, his voice barely above a whisper.

She nodded.

"Down a ways, there's an eagle's nest, and this time

of year sometimes you can see them in it. It's almost magical."

He took her hand again, and they walked along the water's edge, light waves coming only inches from Jake's shoes since he was closer to the water.

Tiffany relaxed, taking in the sights. The sounds of the waves soothed her, and the chattering chipmunks running back and forth entertained her. It was nice that she could walk with Jake in comfortable silence. She didn't know what he was thinking, but at least she didn't have to worry about him yelling at her. He would never do that.

"There it is. Do you see it?" Jake stopped walking, looking up at a cluster of trees.

Tiffany squinted, trying to find the nest. Finally, she saw it nested in a tall tree. "Oh, wow. It's huge."

He squeezed her hand, smiling. "They're not small birds. If we're still enough, they might even come out." He moved closer to her and put his arm around her.

Her heart raced. It was so loud she couldn't hear anything above it. She could smell Jake's woodsy cologne. She pushed herself closer, trying to smell more. He was warm, and even more important, she felt safe. She wanted to stay in his arms, and never leave.

"Do you see that?" he whispered.

Tiffany could feel his warm breath on her ear. She shivered. "What?"

"The top of an eagle head."

The only thing she could focus on was his cologne and the tingling sensation his breath caused.

After a few moments of silence, she was able to focus and she saw the top of the eagle head sticking out of the nest. She could even see part of the beak. "Is that a baby or a grownup?"

"It's an adult." He moved some of her away from her face. "If we stay still, we might get to see it fly." Chills ran down her back with his soft, warm words against her neck.

Jake took her hand with his free one and laced his fingers through hers. They watched as the bird raised its head little by little until they could see the neck. Jake's fingers ran down her bare arm, and then up to her shoulder again. She held her breath, taken in by the beauty of nature and his warm kindness.

He pulled her even closer, nestling his nose against her head. She could feel his breath on her scalp as if he was taking in her scent.

The eagle climbed to the top of the nest, looked around, and then jumped into the air, spreading its wings. The flapping noise even reached Tiffany's ears. She gasped, taken in by it.

Jake moved back to her ear. "It's majestic, isn't it?" he whispered.

Tiffany nodded, still not finding her voice. They watched in silence as the bird became smaller, until it finally disappeared from sight.

"I've never been so close to an eagle before," Tiffany whispered, finally finding her voice.

Jake nodded, moving her hair along with his face. "Sometimes when I'm stressed, I like to come out here. It feels like I'm having complete conversations with some of them, just staring at them as they sit in the nest."

"I believe it. There's something magical about it." Or maybe it was just being with him.

He squeezed her shoulder. "I've always wanted to bring someone here, and I'm glad it's you."

Jake had never taken anyone there before? He'd chosen her? "Me, too."

He rested his head against hers again. Tiffany watched the waves bounce as she felt his soft breaths against her ear and neck. Seagulls flew around chasing each other, and little critters darted around near their feet.

Jake's breath on her neck matched the rhythm of the waves. She closed her eyes, taking in the sounds around her. His heart beat against her back. *If only this could last forever.*

Seventeen

JAKE DIDN'T WANT TO LET go of Elena's hand, but they couldn't stay in the hotel lobby forever. His parents would expect him back at the hospital soon—and he did want to see his dad. He just didn't want the date with Elena to end.

Her hair was a little messy from the wind at the beach. She looked perfect regardless, although he figured she would prefer her hair to be smoothed down.

She let go of his hand and took the flowers to the desk, asking the clerk to put them in a vase and send them to her room. Then she returned to Jake, and he held both of her soft hands in his. "Thank you for going out with me tonight. I had a wonderful time." He stared into her beautiful green eyes. They seemed to grow prettier the more he looked into them.

Her mouth curled into a smile. "So did I. Seeing the eagle was…I don't know. Words fail."

"That they do." He brought her hand to his face and kissed it. "If you're free tomorrow night—"

"I am." Her eyes held the same eagerness he felt.

"You are? What about your car?"

"It'll probably be sitting at Bobby's. But even if it's not..." She looked to the side, as if contemplating what to say. Then she turned back to him and shrugged.

She was so beautiful. Jake stared into her eyes until he realized she was waiting for him to say something. "Well, I'd love to show you another place that tourists don't know about."

Her cheeks flushed. "I'd love that. And if you need help at the shop tomorrow, let me know."

"I really should pay you."

"You can take me out to dinner again." She tilted her head, looking even sweeter.

Jake pretended to think about it. "Hmm....Well, I suppose I could do that. If you insist."

She poked him playfully, and then her face turned serious. "Are you going to visit your dad tonight?"

"Yeah, but I'm having a hard time leaving the present company."

"If you need me to work while you sleep in the morning, I will. I'm serious about helping out."

He shook his head. "I can't ask you to work while I sleep again. I should be there."

"You're not asking. Besides, it gives me something to do."

"Something to do? This town is full of nothing other than things to do."

"It's not really my scene." Elena bit her lip. Jake thought it was adorable. "I'm more comfortable in your shop. It's quaint. I really like it."

"You do? Well, if you want to hang out at the shop, I won't stop you." He stared into her eyes again, not wanting to let her go. Being with her was like a drug—a wonderful escape from reality he wanted more of. "But I should let you get some rest. Speaking of the shop, you worked there for quite a while today."

Elena stared back into his eyes. Could she feel the same way about him? "I probably should go back to my room. I think we're annoying the staff." She looked over to the side.

Jake followed her gaze. A couple of the hotel employees watched them. "They're just jealous." He kissed her hand again. "Goodnight, beautiful lady."

She stared into his eyes, looking embarrassed. Jake should have known she would respond that way to a compliment, even a much deserved one like that. He couldn't get over the intensity of her green eyes. He fought to let go of her hand.

"Goodnight," she finally said. Elena turned around and walked toward the elevators.

Jake couldn't take his eyes off her. When she was out of sight, he finally looked away and walked back to the car, lost in thought. He couldn't feel the ground beneath him. That beautiful and sweet woman actually liked him. Him.

He opened the door, remembering all the times he had liked a girl who ended up choosing one of his brothers. It was the story of his life. He wasn't smart like Brayden, or the alluring bad boy like Cruz. Most girls went for one of them. If not them, than one of his other brothers. Zachary, the mysterious writer. Rafael, the talented fashion designer.

Jake was always the good son, dependable and hardworking. If someone was needed to help out with something, he was the first to step up and get the job done. That made him uninteresting and overlooked. In other words, dull. If someone looked up *boring* in the dictionary, they would find a picture of Jake.

Except for Elena—somehow she actually saw something in him. Jake would have to keep her away from his brothers, especially since they were all likely to come back to town to visit their dad in the hospital.

Did it even matter? She was only passing through. What were the chances of her staying in Kittle Falls? She might not even be in town long enough for him to worry about meeting the other Hunter brothers.

The more time he spent with Elena, the more he wanted. He would almost consider paying Bobby to keep the car longer, but that wouldn't be right. He couldn't do that to her.

Was there any way they could make it work? Would she even consider staying in Kittle Falls? Jake shook his head, laughing bitterly. It wasn't a place people wanted to live. That's why he was the last sibling there. Except for Sophia, who had also never left, but she had been as much a Daddy's girl as Jake was a good son.

What if he went with Elena wherever she was going? He didn't even care where that was, as long as she was there. He could use an adventure, anyway. That would solve his problem of working too many hours with no appreciation and little pay. With all his brothers back in town, they could fight over who was going to run the shop.

He started the car and pulled out of the spot. The days of relying on Jake for everything were over. He was going to step out and have an adventure of his own. It was about time. Someone else could step up and take care of things. Then maybe someone would actually appreciate everything he'd done for the family all those years.

Jake turned on the AC and as it pushed the air around, he got a whiff of Elena's perfume. He took a deep breath, holding onto the scent and imagining her beautiful eyes.

Yes, he needed to make a bold move. Sure, his family needed him, but that was the problem. It was time for him to live *his* life. He pulled into the driveway and stared at the house. It had been his home for his entire life—more than two decades. That was long enough.

He stopped the ignition and got out, slamming the door. The first thing he was going to do was add himself to the payroll and get a car. Then he would get his own place to live—preferably, wherever Elena would be. No more working ridiculously long hours in exchange for just room and board.

When he got inside, he noticed the answering machine blinking the number eight. Eight new messages? He checked his cell phone. No missed calls. They couldn't be an emergency. Or could they? His parents refused to get with the times, so they never called his cell. They had the cell phones Brayden paid for, but almost never used them, relying on landlines.

He pressed play, and found that four of the messages were his mom. Each one more irritated than the last at him for not answering her calls.

Jake slammed his keys on the counter. It wasn't enough that he kept *their* shop going—he was the one paying all their bills—but now she was mad at him for also not being there at her beck and call.

It wasn't like he was avoiding the hospital. He had every intention of going there after his date. It also wasn't like he didn't care about his dad. He was the one who had given up his life to help them out. And he was worried about his dad's health.

Was it so wrong to go out to dinner with a beautiful girl who liked him, and who had helped with their shop that day? They weren't paying her, and she had brought more business to them. Customers bought more things from the front counter than before. When he added up the till at closing, it was their highest grossing day in years.

The phone rang. It was probably his mom again, but he didn't know since they didn't even have caller ID. Jake took a deep breath before picking up the receiver. "Hello?"

"Where have you been?" his mom demanded.

"I had some dinner after closing the shop. Is Dad doing better?"

"Are you going to come to the hospital and see?"

"Yes. I just stopped here first to change my clothes. I heard he's doing a lot better. That's great news."

"Everyone else is here. He's asking about you, Jake."

Jake took a deep breath, and held his voice steady. "And I'm asking about him now. How is he?"

"Why don't you come and see?"

"You make it sound like I haven't done anything all day. The shop—"

"Just hurry up."

"That's where I'm—"

Dial tone.

Jake slammed the receiver down. *Stay calm. She's under stress.*

He leaned against the counter and ran his hands through his hair before going to his room and changing into comfortable clothes.

Jake went back to the car and made his way to the hospital.

When he got to the waiting room, he saw Brayden sitting in a chair. His eyes were closed, and he didn't look comfortable squished into the chair—Brayden was a head taller than the rest of the Hunter brothers.

Jake sat next to him and cleared his throat.

One of Brayden's eyes cracked open. "Jake, buddy. You made it. Mom's been asking about you."

"So I gathered. How's Dad?"

"Appears to have been a stroke. He has better movement than expected, and he's even speaking better than I would have thought. With some time, I think he'll be back to normal—or at least close. It could be a while, though. Months."

Jake groaned. He was glad his dad wasn't in worse shape, but Jake chose the wrong time to stand up about his hours at the shop.

Brayden gave him a curious look. "Are you okay?"

"I'm in a bit of a mood." Jake took a deep breath. "Why aren't you in there?"

"The room's too full. I've been here since last night, so I offered to come out here. I need some rest anyway."

"Go home," Jake said. "A bed would be more comfortable than this. You're going to have a sore neck."

Brayden sat up and stretched. "That's not a bad idea. You should go back and see Dad. I'll catch a ride with you when you leave."

Jake nodded and stood up. "What room is he in?"

"Six-seventy-one." Brayden closed his eyes again,

readjusting himself in the chair.

Jake found his way to his dad's room. It was no wonder Brayden had gone to the waiting room. His mother sat next to the bed, and three other brothers took up the remaining chairs, while an aunt and uncle stood against a wall.

His gaze finally rested on his dad. Jake's heart shattered seeing him in the hospital bed. He pushed his way to the bed. "Dad, are you okay?" Jake took his hand.

His father nodded, although the look in his eyes made Jake wonder if he even recognized him.

"Jake." His dad squeezed Jake's hand.

Relief swept through Jake. He leaned his head against his dad's arm and wept.

Eighteen

~

JAKE FELT A HAND ON his shoulder. He took a deep breath, looked up, and wiped his wet eyes. His aunt Alicia squeezed his shoulder. "He's asked about you a lot. It's good to see you."

Jake stood and gave her a hug. He then said hi to his brothers and turned back to his dad. "I've kept the shop going. It's going better than ever. You don't need to worry about the bills. Everything is going to be just fine." He sniffed, and then wiped his eyes again.

His dad nodded and mumbled something.

"Shh. Don't worry about speaking." Jake kneeled, and slid his hand in his father's. "Get some rest, Dad. We're all here for you, but you don't need to do anything except get better."

"Jake... I love you."

Tears filled Jake's eyes. "Dad, I love you, too." He blinked the tears away, and stared at his father who looked ten years older than he had the other day. He'd already aged prematurely after Sophia's passing, and now he looked old enough to be Jake's grandpa. His hair was significantly grayer and his wrinkles were deeper. Maybe it was only the lighting, and he would look better once at home.

His dad squeezed his hand. One half of his mouth smiled.

Jake's heart ached. "Rest, Dad." He couldn't take his eyes off his dad.

Would he really be okay? He hoped Brayden was right, and that it was only a matter of time. Jake leaned his head against his father's arm again. Would life ever return normal? Or would his family die off one by one? First Sophia, then his dad, followed by his mom? Who next?

He closed his eyes. Soon, conversation started around the room. Jake recognized who spoke, but couldn't make sense of anything said. All he could think about was how he didn't want to lose his dad. He hadn't even had a chance to properly mourn his sister.

After a while, Jake looked up to see his dad sleeping. Jake turned to his mom. "Why don't you let me bring you home? You've been here since last night. Get cleaned up, and sleep in your own bed."

"I can't leave his side."

"You have to take care of yourself. Someone will be here with him at all times." Jake looked around the full room. "Right?"

Cruz sat up and took his coat off, showing his heavily-tattooed arms. "I'll be here, Mom. If he needs anything, I'll get it. Jake's right. You need sleep. I haven't even seen you sit down since I got here."

Zachary stuffed his phone into his pocket, nodding to their mom. "I'm not going anywhere either. Dad's well taken care of, and you know what? He'll be glad you're home resting. He doesn't want you wasting away in that chair."

"They're right, Mom," said Rafael, pulling on the sleeves of his designer shirt—one that he had probably created himself. "The three of us will take care of him. You can send in Brayden, too, when he wakes up. I saw him sleeping in the waiting room."

She looked back and forth at them. "But, I…I can't. What if he wakes up and I'm not here?"

Cruz put an arm around her, and kissed the top of her head. "He'll understand. Do you think he'd want you driving yourself into the ground?"

"Probably not." She frowned.

"You know he wouldn't," Jake said. "Let me drive you home, and then we can return after you've had some sleep."

She leaned against Cruz's shoulder. "Tell him I'll be back soon. Please."

"Of course, Mom. He'll be glad to hear you're taking care of yourself. Besides, if you get sick, how are you going to take care of him? You're taking care of yourself *for* him. The stronger you are, the more you can give him." Cruz nudged her toward the door.

"Point taken." She moved Cruz's arm, and then went to the bed, whispering in her husband's ear. She gave him a kiss, and then turned to Jake. "Do you want me to have one of your brothers drive me? You've hardly spent any time here."

He looked up at the clock. "Dad's sleeping, Mom. Plus, I'm exhausted from running the shop all day." He wasn't about to mention Elena helping him out in the shop. If they thought he could get them free help, his parents wouldn't ever agree to hiring employees.

Cruz raised an eyebrow—the one without piercings. "You're manning the shop all on your own, dude?"

"You see anyone else helping me?" Jake asked, his voice exasperated.

"I mean you haven't hired help?" Rafael asked, looking at Jake like he had lost his mind.

Jake took a deep breath. "I'm not allowed."

"Mom," Zachary said. "How could you guys do that to Jake? It wears me out working there all day with another person."

Cruz turned to their mom. "Let me help Jake with the shop. That way he can spend more time here, or at least get some rest. I've never seen him so ragged. Zachary's right. Jake can't keep this up."

She sighed, looking like she had no fight left in her. "Whatever you boys feel like doing."

Rafael helped her get a jacket on, and then she

hugged everyone else in the room goodbye.

Jake gave Cruz a fist pump to thank him for agreeing to help him with the shop. Then he helped his mom out of the room. They made their way to the waiting room and then said goodbye to the relatives there.

Jake noticed a headache building behind his right eye.

While his mom spoke to one of her sisters, Jake pulled Brayden aside. "Are you sure Dad's going to go back to normal? Did you hear his speech?"

"Of course. With therapy, he'll be back to his old self. He sounds a lot better than most stroke victims."

"But what about his responsibilities?" Jake asked. "He mows the lawn, needs to start running the shop again, and he takes care of the finances. I think he's trying to hide it, but his left arm barely moved."

"Again, therapy." Brayden patted Jake's shoulder. "I'm telling you, all we need is time. Yes, it looks bad now, but he's going to improve each day."

Jake gritted his teeth. "You're a heart doctor, not a stroke expert. Why do you think you know so much about Dad's condition?"

"I've spoken with the doctors here, Jake. They've explained everything to me. It was caught early, and they were able to treat it within a good window of time. We were really lucky."

"Lucky. Right." Jake shook his head. "Our family doesn't have good luck. If we did, Sophia would still be with us and Dad would be home."

"If Sophia taught us anything, it was to appreciate our loved ones while they're with us. Wouldn't you say? Dad's still with us—I don't think we could ask for more at this point."

"What about Sophia? We could ask for her back." Tears stung his eyes. "How much more heartache can this family take?" How much more could *Jake* take?

"Let's hope we don't have to find out," Brayden said. "Why don't you just get Mom home? I'll stay here with Dad as long we need. Both of you look like you need a long night's sleep."

Jake's body ached with exhaustion. "I know I do, and I doubt she's gotten much sleep here."

They walked over to rest of the family, and Jake managed to get his mom into the car and away from the hospital. As soon as they pulled out of the parking lot, she let out a loud cry. "How could this have happened?"

"I don't know, Mom. We're going to have to ask more questions and do our own research."

"First our Sophia, and now this." She sobbed into her hands.

Jake didn't say anything. She likely needed a good cry. Knowing her, she had probably put on a tough face all day at the hospital, trying to be strong for everyone else.

When they got home, he helped her out of the car. "Are you hungry? I can make something to eat." Despite how tired he was, his stomach growled.

"How can I think of food?"

"Because you need to take care of yourself, Mom. How are you going to be any good for Dad if you get sick from not eating or sleeping? We're home so you can recharge, and that's going to take food and rest."

"Oh, all right. If you insist. I think I'll take a shower and get cleaned up first. No need to bring all the hospital germs in our room."

Jake opened the front door. "Perfect. When you get out, I'll have something ready to eat."

She headed for the bathroom while he locked the door. It was strange to be home with only his mom. The house had a quietness that felt wrong. His dad and Sophia should have been there.

The answering machine flashed the number sixteen. He played through them to make sure there wasn't anything important, which there weren't. They were all as he figured. Friends and family calling to find out what was going on. Everyone wanted the details. And they would have to wait.

Zachary, who practically lived online, had posted some updates on social media, but that was never enough. His family was all about personal connections. Forget texting or replying with a comment online when you can call and hear someone's voice.

Jake went through the cupboards and fridge, not finding much he wanted to make. Finally, he found some canned soup buried in the back of the pantry. He dumped the contents into a pot and then made sandwiches. It was at least something to fill their stomachs while they slept.

By the time his mom came into the kitchen, Jake was had just set the table.

"That smells good, Son. Thanks."

"Don't thank me yet. You haven't even tasted it."

Her lips curled upward a little. "Always one to make me smile." She kissed his cheek and then sat down. "Would you bless the meal? Your father usually—" Her voice cracked.

"No problem." He took her hand and prayed over the meal, also asking for an extra blessing on his dad.

They ate the soup and sandwiches in silence.

As he was finishing up, he noticed tears shining in her eyes. "He's going to be okay, Mom. Brayden said it wasn't a bad stroke, and that he should make a full recovery."

"But no one knows. Not even the doctors can see into the future. They just make guesses."

"Based on everything they know and have seen, which is more than we know and have seen. We have to trust them, and Brayden wouldn't lie to us."

She shook her head. "No, he wouldn't. But I won't believe anything until I see it with my own two eyes."

Jake patted the top of her hand. "Tomorrow he'll be doing even better than he was today. I promise."

"You don't know that."

"No, but we have to believe. He needs us to."

She nodded. "You're right. Thanks again for making the food. Would you mind waking me at seven?"

"Do you realize how late it is now?" Jake asked. "You need more sleep than that. Dad has plenty of people to keep him company. It'll make him happy that you're taking care of yourself."

His mom scowled. "Okay. Wake me at nine. What are we going to do about the shop?"

"I'll have to open late. It won't be a big deal."

Her eyes widened.

"Kittle Falls will get along just fine for one morning with us."

"But our finances. We—"

"It'll be fine. I promise. Just get some sleep."

"Nine o'clock." She gave him a stern look.

"Sure thing. Goodnight, Mom." He forced a smile.

She squeezed him tightly, and he returned the embrace.

After cleaning the dishes, Jake climbed into bed, and reached for the alarm. He fell asleep before he touched it. He fell to the pillow, already dreaming.

Nineteen

~

TIFFANY'S ELBOW SLID OFF THE edge of the railing as she stared into the ocean. Her eyes grew heavy, but she couldn't sleep. She readjusted herself, unable to stop thinking about her date with Jake. Everything had been perfect…too perfect?

Would the other shoe drop? Could Jake be hiding something? Everyone had secrets—including her. She hadn't even told him her real name. Sure, Elena was her *new* name, but would it wasn't her real name. Would someone call out "Elena" causing her to turn automatically, knowing it was her? It didn't seem likely.

Guilt stung at her for distrusting him…and keeping such a big secret from him. He was so sweet and caring. He would probably never do the things to her that Trent had done. In fact, he would probably recoil if he knew how long she allowed herself to stay and put up with it.

Jake was everything Trent wasn't, but could her heart handle the risk? Would they both be better off if she simply moved on as planned? It certainly wasn't fair to Jake for her to drag him into her emotional mess. It would probably take years to get over all the damage inflicted by Trent.

She watched people on the beach down below. From the looks of it, the beach was never empty, regardless of the time. At least not in the summer, according to what Jake had said. This far north in California, it was bound to get cold in the winter. Perhaps even as cold as back home. Correction—her old home. She couldn't return there unless Trent was dead or incarcerated, and she couldn't see that happening.

Tiffany noticed a couple sitting by the water's edge far away from the others. They looked cozy, and made her think of Jake. It had felt so good to let go of everything, and just enjoy nature in his arms. Chills ran down her back just thinking of his soft breath on her neck and ears. Oh, how she had wanted him to kiss her. But he had been a perfect gentleman...and that made him all the more desirable.

He was everything she wanted—no, needed. Better, in fact. He was gorgeous, but didn't seem to know it. So many guys thought they were far hotter than they actually were. Men like Trent strutted around like a proud, ugly rooster, thinking they were God's gift to the world. Not Jake, though he easily could have.

Tiffany watched the waves crash, remembering the water near their feet at their secret beach. She could almost feel Jake's warm embrace as she stood on the deck.

It had been so long since she'd allowed herself to feel safe. When Trent wrapped her arms around her, he made Tiffany feel trapped. She always had a mental image of being tied up with a chain and locked up when Trent held her. His grasp was always harsh. Every time he touched her, it felt like a show of ownership instead of a kind embrace…unlike Jake. When he touched her, they seemed to connect on a deep level where words couldn't reach.

They both had their own pain. It was clear the loss of his sister had deeply affected him. Her heart warmed thinking about how sweet that was. He cared so deeply—that much was clear. And he didn't let the pain ruin him. Jake didn't lash out with anger because life wasn't fair. He didn't think the world owed him.

Jake was the kind of guy Tiffany wanted to spend the rest of her life with, if she chose to spend her life with someone. The timing couldn't have been worse. She needed space and time. Probably counseling, and lots of it. Although just the few days already spent away from Trent helped her feel better about everything. Maybe getting away from him was all the professional help she needed.

Tiffany shook her head. That wasn't true, and she knew it. If she was ever going to trust another man with her heart again, it would take years of therapy first. She couldn't get Trent out of her mind. Nearly every thought led back to him and his cruelty. She couldn't stop comparing Jake to him.

She couldn't do that to Jake. He deserved so much more. And he wouldn't want to marry a divorced woman. Not that Tiffany was even divorced yet. Hopefully, though, her grandpa's friends would move the paperwork as fast as promised.

Tiffany turned around and leaned her back against the railing, staring into the hotel room. She was such a liar. When she came clean, Jake would run away, screaming. He wouldn't want someone so…tainted. A bold-faced liar.

Tears ran down her face, and she didn't bother wiping them away. She slid down to the ground and wrapped her arms around her knees. She didn't want to ruin Jake or the wonderful time they'd had.

The best thing to do was walk away—it was the only fair thing to do for Jake. Then they would at least have the memories. If she never loved again, she would at least know she'd been treated well this one week in Kittle Falls. She could hold onto the untainted memories. Every relationship had its problems, and as wonderful as Jake was, they would have a lot of problems because of Tiffany's wounds. She would ruin what they had. It would be better to just have the memories of this short-lived fairy tale.

First thing in the morning, she would march down

to the auto shop and demand the tattooed grease ball move her car to the front of his priority list. She would throw around some threatening phrases if needed. Thanks to Trent, she knew exactly what got under people's skin. She could get Bobby to fix her car in an hour if she really wanted to.

She shuddered. The *last* thing she wanted to do was to act like Trent. Tiffany cried all the harder, shaking. Had he destroyed her so that she wasn't even the sweet girl she had once been? She scooted over to the corner and leaned against it, closing her eyes.

It was becoming clear that she could change her identity, but it didn't make a real difference. She was still broken. More tears fell. Tiffany let them, not wiping them away. She started to feel drowsy, but didn't care. Sleeping in a bed was a luxury she didn't deserve.

What would Trent think if he could see her now? He'd love the sight of her falling asleep on a balcony, not even drunk. He would say she finally realized her worth.

Had she? Had Trent been right about her all along?

While the tears fell down her face, she drifted off to sleep.

A breeze woke her. Tiffany opened her eyes, seeing that it was light out. Her neck and spine ached. Tiffany grabbed the railing and pulled herself up. Looking out over the beach, she stretched her neck, trying to work out the soreness. The beach was crowded, and the stood sun pretty high up in the sky, indicating that it was pretty far into the morning already.

How long had she slept on the deck, curled up against the wall? She stretched her neck the other way and then grabbed her elbow, pulling it tight. A lot of muscles needed attention.

Yawning, she went back into the hotel room. Her eyes watered, blurring her vision. Tiffany wiped them, and then looked in the mirror over the dresser. She looked terrible—hair sticking out every which way, dark circles under her eyes, and lines where her face had been pressed against the wall.

Tiffany grabbed a bowl and poured herself some cold cereal. The milk was running low. If her car wasn't ready soon, she would need to get more, and before she did, Tiffany would need to figure out what to say to Jake.

There was a part of her that wanted to stick around just a little longer to spend some more time with him, greedy for more of what they'd shared the night before. But she wanted to get away so she didn't have a chance to ruin what they had. She just wanted to keep the memories they had made.

Yet part of her wanted to stay and see if they had a chance.

She looked into the mirror at her green eyes. "You're impossible." Staring into her reflection, she knew what she had to do. Though she'd changed a lot over the last couple years with Trent, she was still the kind of person who did the right thing. Right now, that meant not stringing Jake along.

There was no way she could commit to anything, and if she let things progress, she was being unfair to him. He deserved someone who could give him better. She was damaged goods with too many secrets and not enough to offer. Anytime he became irritated, she would jump or cower. Jake should have someone who would be able to handle normal emotions.

Tiffany had even jumped away from her grandpa when he got angry a couple times, and he was the safest man in the world. She knew deep within her soul that he wouldn't do a thing to hurt her, yet she couldn't help flinching.

She got into the shower and freshened up. Her clothes needed to be washed, and she still looked like she'd had a rotten night's sleep. At least makeup could cover that.

Tiffany grabbed some red lipstick, dabbed it on the dark circles and then rubbed it in, covering it with foundation. Perfect. She'd learned the trick in high school after pulling many all-nighters, and it worked every time.

Just as she dabbed on the last bit of makeup, she heard her phone. Hoping it was Jake, she ran to check. She had a new text from Grandpa. *I need to fix some paperwork, Tiff. Where are you staying?*

She read it over several times. Grandpa had told her numerous times he didn't want to know where she was. Why would he ask that now?

You know I'm not supposed to tell you. Is this a test?

Tiffany waited for another text for a minute, and then her phone sang again.

Ha, ha. Yeah. You passed. We'll talk later, honey.

Okay. She put the phone back in her purse, shaking her head. What was that all about?

When she was finally ready, she walked to the auto shop. Her car was actually in the garage. It wasn't raised like the others. Could that actually mean it was ready? Her heart raced as she walked inside. Was she nervous about finding out that she would be leaving or staying? She wasn't even sure.

Bobby sat at the desk, flipping through paperwork. As usual, all the seats in the waiting room were full. Tiffany walked over to the desk, putting on her best irritated voice. "Is my car ready yet?"

He looked up. A smile spread across his face. "Ah, Elena. We've got it lined up. Did you see it's finally in the garage? As soon as we finish one, we'll get to yours."

Not only was it not ready, but given their speed, it could be another week before she could drive it away. She made sure to keep her voice steady. "Do you know when it'll be ready?"

"That all depends on when we get started, and what's wrong with it. If it's something simple, you could have it back after lunch. I wouldn't hold my breath, though."

"Don't worry, I won't." She spun around and left the shop. The sun felt even hotter than it had only minutes before.

Tiffany fanned herself as she made her way to Jake's shop. If she was going to be in town anyway, she wanted to spend her time with Jake. She pulled on the door, and when it wouldn't budge, her hand slipped from the handle, breaking a nail. She looked at it, seeing that it was broke below the line, and she stuck the nail in her mouth to stop the pain before it started.

"You okay?"

She turned around to see Dimitri. "Broke a nail. I'll be fine. Jake hasn't opened the shop yet?"

"He hasn't been in all day."

"I'm not surprised. He went to see his dad at the hospital last night. He probably didn't get much sleep."

Dimitri nodded, looking serious for a change. "I've seen most of his brothers back in town—it must be pretty bad. They don't usually come it back home, except for the holidays."

Tiffany frowned. "Well, if he does come in, can you tell him I stopped by? I can help with the shop again if he needs me." Though if he hadn't opened the shop, they obviously weren't too worried about getting help.

Even though she hadn't met his dad, she couldn't help worrying something was wrong.

"Will do. You could always stop by his house and—"

"No. I don't want to disturb him. He probably needs his sleep. See you around."

Twenty

~

BRIGHT SUNLIGHT STREAMED DOWN ON Jake's face from the newly opened curtains, waking him. He covered his eyes, blocking the sun, and glared at his mom. "What gives?"

"You were supposed to wake me three hours ago." His mom narrowed her eyes. "What will your father think?"

Jake sat up, rubbing his eyes. "That we're taking care of ourselves, and the house. He'll be happy, and we know he hasn't been alone for even a minute. Cruz, Rafael, Zachary, and Brayden all promised to stay with him, remember? They all want you to get much needed sleep, too. And I'm sure everyone else will be there, as well. Why don't we get some breakfast, and then I'll take you back before I open the shop?"

Her face softened. "I'll make the food this time. You get cleaned up."

Jake showered and got dressed. When he came out, he smelled bacon and eggs—his favorite breakfast food.

"Sit down and eat." She handed him a piece of ba-con.

They ate in silence, and then Jake dropped her off at the hospital entrance.

When he got to the shop, Jake turned the key in the doorknob. He didn't want to be there, but at least it wouldn't be all day for a change. Cruz was going to take over after going home and sleeping. He'd been up all night at the hospital as promised. Jake and he had left the hospital at the same time. Jake to the shop, and Cruz on his motorcycle ready to sleep in his old bed.

"There you are," Dimitri said from behind.

Jake turned around. "Hey there."

"I've never seen your shop open so late."

"I don't want to talk about it," Jake said. "Sorry, friend."

"Does it have anything to do with the pretty girl?" Dimitri asked, the corners of his mouth twitching.

Jake leaned his head against the window on the door. If he'd gotten up earlier, he would have seen her. He'd dreamed of holding her by the shore all night. "Elena came by?"

"She looked quite disappointed. I think she wanted to see you." Dimitri grinned. "She likes you."

"Did she say anything?"

Dimitri put a finger to his chin and looked up. "Yeah. She said she could help you out with the shop."

"Thanks, pal." Jake went inside and locked the door

behind him, getting the register ready for the day. As soon as he flipped the sign from *Closed* to *Open* and unlocked the door, people poured in. He was so busy he didn't have time to even think about calling Elena, though he wanted nothing more.

After the lunch rush, things finally fell into a lull. Jake counted the till, surprised to see they had earned more money when opening late than when he went in early. It had to be from Elena redecorating. He should hire her to fix up the rest of the shop. He slammed the register shut, and then heard the bell.

"This place hasn't changed a bit." Cruz walked around the perimeter of the shop. "I feel like I've entered a time warp, dude. Between this and the house. It's like everything is frozen in my high school days." He wandered a bit, until he stopped in front of the counter. He did a double-take. "Never mind. This is different. Everything else is frozen in time, though."

"Try living it," Jake muttered.

Cruz leaned against the counter. "You ought to get out of this town. There's a whole big world out there."

Jake shrugged. "You know how it goes. They need me."

"Are you afraid to leave?" Cruz stared into Jake's eyes.

"Watch it, or you'll find yourself with a black eye."

Cruz laughed. "And you'll end up with your head pinned between my side and my arm."

"I'm not scared to leave Kittle Falls, Cruz. Someone has to stick around with Mom and Dad, not to mention this pitiful shop."

"Pitiful? It has character."

"You mean the time warp?" Jake arched an eyebrow.

"Something like that. Well, dude, get outta here and do whatever you need to. And I don't mean going to the hospital, either. I just talked with Brayden, and he says the number of relatives has doubled since I left this morning. You need a break from everything—this shop and taking care of everyone. It's not your job to keep the family running."

Was that how everyone saw him?

The bell rang above the door. Jake stepped out from behind the counter, patting it. "She's all yours, Brother."

Cruz took his place and looked around. He took his hoodie off and slung it over a chair. "This is the same register they bought when I was six."

Jake shrugged. "You know them. If it's not broke...."

Cruz looked past Jake and grinned, standing taller. "Hello, there," he said, obviously talking to a pretty girl. "Can I help you?"

"I'm here to see Jake."

Jake spun around. "Elena."

She smiled. "I came by to see if you'd opened the shop yet. Do you need any help? Or do you have some already?" Elena looked over at Cruz.

"That's my brother, Cruz. He's giving me the afternoon off."

"Yeah, but you'd better come back and close for me. I can't remember how to do that." He turned to Elena. "It's nice to meet you. And you are?" Cruz shot Jake a look, obviously wanting to know their relationship status.

Jake stepped closer to Elena.

"I'm Elena." She shook Cruz's hand. "Nice to meet you, too. How's your dad?"

"He's a fighter. If he has his way, he'll be back home tomorrow, painting the walls or something crazy like that."

Elena laughed. "Must be where Jake gets his ability to work here by himself day after day."

"No doubt. Well, you two crazy kids get outta here." Cruz gave Jake an approving look, obviously liking Elena.

"Thanks again," Jake said.

"Maybe I'll even hire a few people while you're away. Not sayin' I'll train them or anything, but hey, help is help."

"You do that." Jake took Elena's hand. He loved how smooth her skin felt against his. He rubbed his thumb along her palm, his mood drastically improving.

She smiled, a little color filling her cheeks. Her sweetness was refreshing.

They walked toward the door, and just as Jake opened it, Elena turned around and waved to Cruz. "Bye."

"Have fun with my brother."

Elena giggled, and then they walked out into the warm sunshine.

Dimitri gave Jake a thumbs-up from behind his newspaper stand.

"Want to walk along the shore?" Jake asked, inching closer to her as they walked in the warm sun. "We can go the opposite direction of the crowds."

She squeezed his hand. "I'd love that."

They walked to the beach in a comfortable silence. It seemed like she appreciated the quiet as much as he did. When they reached the water, he turned to the left, going toward the non-touristy part of town. About a mile away sat a quaint beach enjoyed by the locals, most of whom were busy working right then.

"I had a lot of fun last night," she said.

"Me, too." He let go of her hand and put his arm around her shoulders. "Spending time with you is such a breath of fresh air."

"I couldn't agree more." She looked troubled.

"Is everything okay?" Maybe she would open up and tell him what she was running from, if that was indeed what was going on.

Elena shrugged, paused, and then nodded. They went back to walking in silence. Jake relaxed the farther they walked. The sounds of waves crashing against the sand had a calming effect—it always had since he was a boy.

He wished he could think of a way to get her to open up, but feared he would push her away instead.

"We're almost there," he said. "The area should be nearly empty. If we're lucky, we'll have it to ourselves."

She looked ahead. "If it's anything like the beach last night, I'm sure it'll be perfect."

They rounded a corner, and the big, empty beach welcomed them.

Elena stopped. "It's beautiful. I can't believe no one's here."

"Not many want to make the hike. Most of the tourists expect the crowded, festive beach. They're happy with it."

She continued to look around, and then turned to Jake. "Do you mind if I take my shoes off and walk in the water?"

"Mind? I'll join you." He couldn't help smiling. With any luck, he would get to see more of her playful side. He had seen little sparks of it, but being barefoot on the sand, she might burst out of her shell.

Elena slid off her sandals while Jake took off his sneakers and socks. He rolled up his pants, regretting the clothing choice. He thought he'd be in the air-conditioned hospital later, and hadn't wanted to be cold then. They set their shoes on a bench, and then Elena burst into a run for the water.

"Hey!" Jake laughed, running after her.

She turned and looked at him, not slowing until she reached the water.

He caught up easily since she nearly stopped at the shore. "Are we done playing chase?"

"I just wanted to feel the ocean." She looked away from him, and down at her feet and wiggled her toes around the water, bringing sand over them.

"There's nothing like it." Jake wiggled his toes, too. He hadn't done that in years. The warm waves splashed over their feet, onto their ankles.

Elena broke out into another run, surprising Jake. He could hear her beautiful laugh over the waves. He chased her, splashing saltwater onto his pants. She was actually pretty fast, and unfortunately, he was rather out of shape. Working out hadn't been on his priority list in a long time.

Not since the days he came here with his friends before Sophia got sick.

He finally caught up to Elena, and tapped her shoulder. She whipped around and poked his arm. "You're it—again."

"Hey, not fair." Not fair? When was the last time he'd said that? He couldn't help laughing. Somehow, she managed to bring out *his* carefree side—he hadn't thought it still existed.

Jake watched Elena's hair fly back behind her as she

ran. His heart swelled, warming. Whatever that girl was doing to him, he wanted more of it—and her. He had to find a way to talk her into staying in town.

He kicked his feet into gear, and went after her as fast as he could. She grew closer until he could almost reach her. Without warning, she turned around, and they crashed into each other.

They both burst into laughter. She surprised him by wrapping her arms around him. "Looks like you got me."

"Or did you get me?" Jake put his arms around her, pressing his face against her hair. He breathed in her sweet scent. She was perfect.

Elena turned, keeping herself pressed against him. She leaned her head against his shoulder and they looked out over the water, watching the waves and the birds flying.

"This is the best," she said.

"It sure is." Jake loved having her there in his arms with the water lapping at their feet. It was wonderful to pretend he had no worries, and that everything in his sight and arms was all the world contained. He longed for a reality this wonderful, and he would take what he could get of it.

Twenty-One

~

TIFFANY PRESSED HER CHEEK AGAINST Jake's, taking in his scent. He smelled of soap and aftershave, and mixed with the ocean air, it was heavenly. She sniffed again, unable to get enough.

He tightened his grip around her, and she loved being in his arms. It felt so good to be with someone so kind and sweet...so safe. In school, she had thought safe boys were boring, but now she wanted nothing more. She felt like he would protect her and suddenly couldn't understand why that morning she had been planning on leaving town.

Time seemed to stand still, and she didn't want to think about anything from the past or future. She would have been happy to stay there forever in his warm embrace.

A breeze picked up, and her hair flew around, whipping both of them in the face.

Jake let go of her and wiped it away from his face. "Now I know why I never had long hair."

Tiffany laughed. "Sorry." She pulled an elastic band from her wrist and tied her hair behind her. "That should fix it."

He looked disappointed. "I like your hair down. It's beautiful."

She felt her cheeks warm up. "I could take it down." Tiffany looked into his eyes, and neither said anything. She parted her lips to say something, but nothing would come. His gaze was so intense, she could see the same desire in them that she felt—to stay on the beach together forever.

Jake ran his fingertips down Tiffany's face, giving her chills despite the hot sun. He continued staring into her eyes, and his fingers lingered near her chin.

Tiffany let out a breath, realizing she'd been holding it in.

Finally, Jake spoke. "You don't need to change your hair. Either way, you're gorgeous. You could never look anything less than perfect."

Her cheeks burned, and then tears blurred her vision. She couldn't remember the last time anyone said she was pretty—much less gorgeous or perfect—and it had been even longer since she felt attractive.

Not only did she believe Jake meant every word, but she felt like it might be true. She blinked, tears spilling onto her cheeks.

Concern filled Jake's eyes, and he wiped the tears from her face. "What's the matter? Did I say something wrong?"

She shook her head. "I...I just.... It's been a long time since anyone has said anything so nice to me. That's all." She looked away, more tears escaping.

"What about the things I've said to you before? I thought I told you how attractive you are. Didn't I?"

Tiffany's cheeked heated even more. "I meant before I met you." She swallowed, hoping to get rid of the lump in her throat. Another tear escaped.

Jake wiped where it had fallen. "What happened? Who hurt you so badly?" He put his fingertips on her chin and turned her head so she was looking at him.

Her heart pounded in her ears, drowning out the sounds of the ocean. Did she dare open up to him? It might be healing to talk to him about what had happened. Deep down, she knew she could trust him. And if he did run away screaming, at least she wouldn't have to see him again.

"You don't have to talk about it," he whispered, rubbing the back of his hands along her face.

Tiffany took a deep breath and looked away from him. Her hands shook, and her heart pounded harder, feeling like it would jump out of her chest. Adrenaline rushed throughout her body.

Jake took her hand and kissed it. "We can talk about something else. The—"

"I was married, Jake. I'm sorry I didn't tell you before. He treated me horribly."

"You have nothing to apologize for." He stared into her eyes. "I'm sorry that jerk didn't know what a good thing he had." Jake pulled her into a tight hug.

Tiffany felt a rush of relief at his understanding. Tears filled her eyes and spilled onto his shirt. Her entire body shook in his arms, but he didn't let go. He held her tighter, and she listened to his strong heartbeat as she cried harder than she had in a long time. The last thing she wanted was to give Trent the satisfaction of knowing that he could break her, so she had built a wall around herself.

Now with Jake, it crumbled all around her. Her grandpa had been right. She had shut everyone out, pushing all of her friends away. Now she had no friends. Maybe if she would've kept them and opened up, she might not have had to leave her hometown. But then she wouldn't have met Jake. Part of her wanted to stay in Kittle Falls with him…maybe more than part if she was honest with herself.

Finally, the tears slowed, and she gained control of herself. She wiped her face dry before looking back at Jake. She sighed, not having the words to express how she felt.

He pulled some hair away from her face that had come loose from the ponytail and tucked it behind her ear. He was both gentle and strong at the same time. His strength was one she could trust.

"I'll never be harsh with you, Elena. Ever. I promise."

She opened her mouth to speak, but again found words lacking. Her lips trembled.

He touched her mouth gently with his fingertip, and then moved closer. Tiffany's heart pounded in her chest, so loud it was all she could hear. Jake moved his finger out of the way in time to press his soft, warm lips on hers.

Tiffany's heart nearly leaped out of her chest. She closed her eyes, taking in more of his wonderful scent.

Jake pulled away slowly, and Tiffany opened her eyes, holding his eye contact. They stared into each other's eyes for a moment until Jake pulled her close again, holding her tight.

"I'm serious, Elena. You'll always be safe with me. I won't ever let anyone mistreat you."

Tiffany felt like she would melt in his arms. She shook again, and he tightened his grip around her.

"Let it all out," he whispered.

She wrapped her arms around him, holding on tight. "Thank you."

He slid a hand down to the small of her back. "I hate to see you in so much pain. You want me to find that jerk and beat him up?"

Tiffany couldn't help laughing. She looked at Jake, who smiled.

"I'll do it if you want me to."

"No. But I appreciate the offer." She stared into his

eyes, wishing he would kiss her again. She didn't have the nerve to kiss him just yet.

Jake pointed to a nearby bench. "Want to sit?"

Tiffany nodded, and then they walked over and sat after dusting the sand off the seat. He put his arm around her, holding her close. They watched the waves without saying anything. Tiffany just loved being near him. She wasn't bothered by the hot sun or the breeze blowing sand in their faces.

Jake spoke up. "When I was growing up, my family used to spend a lot of time down here. My parents would hire students to run the shop, and they would bring us here for hours every day. Some of my best memories are here. My sister used to tease me to no end. Her favorite was practical jokes. If I wasn't careful, I would end up with a hair full of sand…or worse." He squirmed next to her.

"Your shorts?" Tiffany asked, trying to hold back a smile.

Jake grimaced. "More than I care to admit."

Tiffany giggled. "I wish I could have met her."

"Me, too. You would have loved each other." Jake paused, looking thoughtful. "Aside from being devious, she was also the most wonderful person. Generous to a fault, and always finding the best in people." He took a deep breath, his eyes shining with tears. "She always had friends and boyfriends. Everyone wanted to be Sophia's friend, you know? I was the lucky one, though. Her favorite brother. There wasn't anyone who could come between us." He cleared his throat.

"Sounds like she was pretty lucky, too." Tiffany leaned against his shoulder.

"I hope so." His voice cracked. "I was glad to be able to take care of her when she got sick. Mom and Dad had to work long, hard hours because the insurance only covered so much of her treatments. I had no real responsibilities at the time, so I was able to be with her just about every waking hour. My parents appreciated it, knowing that someone was there for her when they couldn't be. I don't think they even slept. When they weren't working, they took over taking care of her so I could sleep." He sighed. "We all really thought she was going to make it. If we knew she was going to take a turn for the worse, I know they would have spent more time with her. I kind of feel bad that I had so much more time with her than anyone else."

"I bet she knew how loved she was." Tiffany took his hand and gave a squeeze. "It's obvious how much you miss her."

Tears spilled onto his face, and his nose grew red. "I think she knew." His voice wavered. Jake leaned against her and shook. Tiffany wrapped her arms around him, glad to give him the same support he'd just given her.

Was he as broken as she? Only for different reasons entirely?

After a bit, he sat up, wiping his eyes. "I hate that

she's not here, you know? It just isn't fair. This world is full of jerks. Why not one of them?"

"You're right, and it totally sucks." People like Trent would probably live to be a hundred, while sweet people like Sophia never got to see thirty. "She should be here right now throwing sand at you. With my help." Tiffany kissed his cheek.

Jake laughed, wiping tears. "I'd love nothing more."

Tiffany leaned down and scooped up sand. "In honor of Sophia."

"Wait, what…?" Jake looked at her in confusion.

Laughing, she pulled out the back of his collar and dumped the sand down his shirt.

He jumped up, hollering. "I didn't mention that I always got her back." He gave her a devilish look, and shook his shirt, sending sand in all directions.

"Go ahead and try." Tiffany ran toward the water. She could hear his footsteps not far behind. Turning her head, she saw a pile of sand in his hands. She picked up her speed, but as her right foot sunk into the wet sand, she stumbled. Her knees landed first, and she barely had enough time to put out her hands to stop her face from smashing into the wet sand.

Tiffany rolled over to see Jake standing over her with the sand.

"No!" she shrieked, covering her face. "You wouldn't."

He laughed, and she moved her arms to see him

looking charming and devious. Her heart skipped a beat. Two equally strong emotions ran through her. Dread for the coming sand and adoration for the gorgeous and sweet man about to dump it on her. She put her hands over her face again.

"For Sophia," he said.

Tiffany closed her eyes. Then she felt the breeze of the sand landing near—not on—her head. She turned and looked at the pile just out of reach, and then up to Jake.

He shrugged. "You're sandy enough as it is." He grabbed her hands and pulled her up. "It's going to take a while to get all that out of your hair." He dusted the top of her head.

"I'm not worried about it." She smiled at him, moving closer to him.

Jake pulled her into an embrace. "Thanks for giving me a new memory out here. I needed a new good one."

"Maybe we'll have to come back and make more."

They held each other's eye contact, and then Jake leaned closer, placing his lips on hers again.

Twenty-Two

~

TIFFANY STOOD OVER THE SINK, scowling at herself. Despite washing her hair three times, sand still fell from her hair. She was glad Jake hadn't dumped any on her, or she would have never gotten it all out—not that she would have traded the time spent with him for anything. Sand was only a minor inconvenience given the wonderful time they'd had.

Her heart fluttered thinking about him. After opening up to him, and then him to her, she really wanted to stay in town longer. It wasn't like Trent would find her there in Kittle Falls. She could have a sweet summer romance, and then who knew what would happen after that? All she knew was that she needed more of Jake.

Tiffany got comfortable on the bed, and closed her eyes, replaying every moment she'd spent with Jake. Why hadn't she met Jake first? She could have saved herself a lot of heartache, and she could have been there alongside him when he took care of Sophia.

She grew drowsy and fell into a deep sleep, dreaming of how things could be better now that she'd met Jake.

When the phone woke Tiffany, she didn't feel any more rested, but she had hope. The last couple of years were full of regret, but that didn't mean the rest of her life had to be. She stretched, and then tried to find her phone.

She followed the sound, finding it on the floor underneath a pillow and some blankets. Tiffany must have kicked all of those off in her sleep. By the time she tried answering, she had missed the call. Scrolling around the screen, she saw two missed calls.

Her blood ran cold when she saw both were from an unknown number. It was local to her hometown. Tiffany recognized the area code and prefix. There were no messages. Her hand shook as she stared at the screen.

Tiffany gripped the phone, her knuckles turning white. Could Trent have found the number? Her new identity? Did he know she was in Kittle Falls?

Breathe, she told herself. Maybe it was just a wrong number. Someone trying to reach the person who last had the number. That made more sense than Trent having the number. No one other than her grandpa had it, and even if someone went through his phone, they wouldn't know it was Tiffany because he filed it under Elena.

She took several deep breaths trying to calm herself. There was no reason to worry. There had to be a good reason for those two calls, and later she'd probably laugh about it.

Although, she didn't find any humor yet. Staring at the number, she contemplated calling it back. What if something had happened to her grandpa? One of his poker buddies could have been going through the list of contacts on Grandpa's phone. But if that was the case, why wasn't the number from Grandpa's phone?

Finally, Tiffany decided not to call back, but if *they* called back, she would answer. She slid it into her pocket and then dumped everything out of her bags. She was growing more disorganized the longer she spent at the hotel. All of her clothes were dirty and wrinkled. There was nothing decent to change into.

She couldn't see Jake in any of these. It was time to do laundry or go shopping. The hotel had to have some sort of laundry facilities. She looked over the mess on her bed. Maybe she should look into apartments. With it being a tourist town, she might find a studio she could rent on a month-by-month basis. She could stay a month and see how things went with Jake. If they continued having fun, she could stay another month. If it didn't work out, then she'd just move on like planned. The thought of it not working out hurt.

Tiffany threw the clothes in one bag, and everything else in the other. Then she scrolled through the phone until she found local real estate. She had just found an apartment building with studios when the phone rang.

It scared her, and she nearly dropped the phone. It was the same number from earlier. Her heart skipped a beat, but she pressed accept. "Hello?"

"Elena?" asked a male voice.

"Who's this?" Tiffany asked.

"Vinny. Why do you have Alfy's wife's name?"

Tiffany gasped. "Is Grandpa okay?"

"Wait. Tiffany?"

"Yeah. It's a long story. Is he okay?"

"No, sweets, he's not."

The room spun around her. "What...what do you mean?"

"He's in the hospital. Are you nearby?"

Tiffany sat down on the bed. "I can get there. But first, tell me what happened."

"His maid service came by this morning, and found him slumped over the couch. He was unconscious, but had a pulse and bruises. She called 911, and he's been at the hospital ever since. They found a weird cocktail of drugs in his system, so given that and the bruises, it looks like he was poisoned."

A horrible sound escaped from Tiffany's throat. "Is he going to be okay?"

"They say he should be. Whoever did this to him knew what they were doing."

Tears filled her eyes. "Does anyone know who it was?"

"We've all picked up enemies over the years, but

none of us knew of any recent ones for Alfy."

"Except one." Tiffany clenched her fists.

"Who?" Anxiety filled Vinny's voice.

"Trent."

"Your Trent? Hold it. That car I found Alfy—that was for you? Are you running from Trent?"

"I—"

"Everything makes sense now. Your absence, the poisoning. Trent's why you've been acting like a scared church mouse the last couple years, isn't it?"

"He—"

"And now you're using Elena's identity. Frankie probably set you up with a new driver's license, didn't he?"

"Stop." Tiffany steadied her voice. "Figure this all out later. I'm not entirely sure how Grandpa put all of this together for me, but I need a plane ticket back to Seattle. Like, now."

"Right. Right. Where from, Tiff?"

"Is your phone secure?"

Vinny laughed. "You have to ask, sweets?"

"Actually, yeah. I'm in northern California."

"I'll set it up. Get yourself to the airport as soon as you can. I'll text you the flight details. How far away from the airport are you?"

Tiffany thought about the route she had traveled. "I don't remember seeing an airport. I'm not sure. Sorry, Vinny."

"No problem. Where are you?"

Even though the phones were supposed to be secure, she didn't want to say. Not even Grandpa had wanted to know where she was, and he understood the importance of Tiffany keeping quiet. She tried to remember some of the town names she saw on her way to Kittle Falls. "I'm in Westerfield." It was about a half an hour away.

"Westerfield?" He muttered some numbers. "Okay. We'll give an hour for traffic. Hurry up."

"Will do. Thanks, Vinny."

"Anything for you, sweets. I'll keep my eyes open for Trent, too."

"Thanks. I appreciate it." Vinny's eyes meant a network of guys around the area looking for him, also. Tiffany ended the call.

She remembered the strange texts from Grandpa. What if they hadn't been from him at all? If Trent had poisoned Grandpa, he could have texted from his phone, too. Her stomach twisted in knots.

There was no way she could leave her grandpa to languish in the hospital. She needed to see him even if it meant possibly running into Trent. Vinny and his friends would be able to keep her safe. They were already looking for Trent.

Shaking, Tiffany picked up the hotel phone, asking the front desk to call her a taxi. She grabbed her bags and realized she probably wouldn't be able to take half the stuff on the plane. She dumped out the bag with the non-clothes items and threw away everything the airlines would confiscate.

She grabbed her purse, threw the bag of clothes over her shoulder, and hurried to the elevator. When she got to the lobby, Tiffany was irritated to see a line at the front desk. There hadn't been a line the entire time she'd been there, and now there was one?

Muttering to herself, Tiffany went to the back of the line. She fidgeted, hoping it wouldn't take too long.

The lady at the front of the line raised her voice, complaining about a wrong date. This was going to take forever.

Someone tapped her shoulder. Tiffany turned around to see a hotel employee. She smiled at Tiffany. "Are you checking out? If so, I can help you over there." The lady pointed to another corner of the lobby where a smaller counter was.

"Yes, please," Tiffany begged. "I have a bit of an emergency to get home to."

"I thought you looked worried. Follow me, hon."

Less than five minutes later, Tiffany climbed into the back of a taxi.

"Where to?"

Tiffany looked at her phone to see Vinny's text. "Arcata-Eureka Airport."

"Okay. Hang on." The driver hit the gas before Tiffany had a chance to buckle in.

The traffic wasn't too bad, so it didn't take long. She was surprised at how small the airport was. It was no Sea-Tac.

"I'm probably going to have to take a connecting flight."

"More than likely. The only direct flight from here is San Francisco. Otherwise, it'll just take you to one of the larger local airports."

"Wonderful," she grumbled. That would only make her travels longer. Tiffany swiped the credit card and got out. She was relieved to find that she only had a short wait for her flight. Checking her phone, she found another text from Vinny with the remaining flight info.

Twenty-Three

~

"TELL ME MORE ABOUT ELENA." Cruz sipped a cup of coffee, staring at Jake from across the counter. Some customers entered the shop, but neither brother paid any attention.

Jake couldn't hold back a smile. "She's amazing."

Cruz grinned and reached across the counter, punching Jake in the arm. "Look at you. What's she like?"

"Beautiful, smart, funny, and sweet." Jake sighed.

"Oh, come on, bro. That tells me nothing. I could tell you that from my short interaction with her. I want to know more about the woman who finally got your attention."

"What's that supposed to mean?" Jake asked, wondering if he should be annoyed.

"Dude, you've been so busy the last few years, you've barely gone on a date, much less hooked up with anyone."

Jake made a face. "I'm not into hooking up. If I'm

going to spend time with someone, I want it to be meaningful."

"Yeah, yeah. I know, but that's the problem. Things always come up, and you just need some fun."

"Well, I've been having a blast with Elena. Why are you suddenly so interested in my love life?"

"I hate seeing my baby brother miserable."

"You also know I hate it when you call me that."

Cruz walked around the counter, put his hand on top of Jake's head, and messed up his hair.

"Would you stop?" Jake tried to fix his hair.

"You could try thanking me for taking over the shop so you could go to the beach with her." He stared at Jake's shirt. "Is that sand under your shirt?" He wiped at Jake's neckline.

Jake stepped back. "I forgot how annoying you are."

Cruz put the coffee cup down. "Really? I hired two assistants for you. One's even cute."

"Mom and Dad are going to freak—you realize that, don't you?" Jake shook his head.

"What are they going to do? If they're not here, they can't do nothing. Right?"

"I guess. When do they start?"

"Bella—she's the cute one—will be here in the morning. Then at lunch she leaves and Calvin will be here all afternoon. He's not cute, but he seems responsible." Cruz shrugged, taking another sip of coffee.

"We'll give it a try. So, do you have anyone special

in your life?" Jake raised an eyebrow.

"Not with my schedule, yo. You know I'm working at the tat parlor on the weekends?"

"Yeah."

"I ain't got time for no relationship. Then I'd just hear about how I'm never home, and blah, blah, blah. Who needs that? Not me." Cruz rubbed a new tattoo on his arm. Jake figured it probably itched.

"As long as you're happy, Cruz. So, have you heard anything new about Dad today?"

"Nope. If something was wrong, they'd call."

Music sounded as both of their phones rang.

Cruz looked at his screen and scowled. "Damn. Jinxed that."

A group of customers walked over.

Cruz slammed his fist on the counter. "You take the call, and then tell me what's going on. I'll get the customers."

Jake tapped accept and hurried to the back room, closing the door behind him. "Aunt Alicia?" he said into the phone.

"Is Cruz with you?" his aunt asked.

"Yeah. We're at the shop. What's going on?"

"You boys need to get over here to the hospital right away." Her voice shook.

Jake's stomach dropped to the floor, and he sat in the nearest chair. "Why? You need to tell me what's going on."

"His blood pressure dropped, and then he had seizures. The doctors sent us to the waiting room, but your mom and you kids need to get in to see him as soon as the staff will let you in. He needs to be surrounded by everyone he loves."

Everything disappeared around Jake, and he took several deep breaths. "I thought he was getting better. Why is this happening?"

"I don't know what's going on, but you and Cruz need to close shop and get over here. Now."

"Okay. We'll be right over." Jake ended the call, and looked at the phone in disbelief. "How can Dad be getting worse?"

The shop sounded busy on the other side of the door. Either they would have to wait until it cleared out, or they would need to kick everyone out. He stood up and stumbled.

"Get a hold of yourself," Jake scolded himself. He took some deep breaths, and focused on what was in front of him. He had to walk out into the store without looking like a drunken fool. Jake took one more deep breath before walking again. One foot in front of the other. It was that simple.

He stumbled a couple times before reaching the door, but after opening it, he was able to walk normally.

Cruz looked over at him, raising an eyebrow, as he handed a receipt to a customer. "Is everything okay?" He looked like he knew that answer already.

Jake shook his head. "We're going to have to close the shop and get over to the hospital."

Cruz swore, and then he clapped his hands over his head. "Sorry everyone," he yelled, "but we have to close right now. We have a family emergency. If you have something in your hands right now, get to the registers. Otherwise, exit promptly. We hope to be open again later today."

Groans and mumbles echoed throughout the store. Jake went over to the doors and turned the sign to *Closed*. Then he went around to the counter and opened up the second register. It creaked in complaint since it was so rarely used.

Jake and Cruz spent the next fifteen minutes ringing everyone up before closing the tills.

"Don't tell me what's wrong," Cruz said. "I'll drive, and I need to keep a level head."

"Yeah, sure." Jake took the money from Cruz and put it in the safe in the back room.

They went to the hospital in relative silence. The only sounds were of the rock music Cruz had put on. Jake worried about what shape their dad would be in when they got there. Would their family have to deal with another death? His heart nearly leaped into his throat. He wasn't sure he could deal with that, and he knew his mom couldn't.

When Cruz pulled into a parking spot, he turned to Jake. "Okay, now tell me what's going on."

Jake cleared his throat. "He had a seizure, and everyone was kicked out of the room. Something about his blood pressure, too." He pulled on his hair. "Aunt Alicia barely told me anything."

"He's alive, though?"

"Yeah."

"Okay, good. Let's get up there."

They hurried to the waiting room. Their family had taken over and filled it. Jake went over to Brayden. "What's going on?"

Brayden's eyes shone with tears. "That's what we're waiting to find out." He put his arms around Jake and squeezed.

Jake returned the hug and then stood back. "What happened?"

Brayden wiped his eyes. "Everything was going well. Dad was talking again, like last night." Brayden blinked a few times, and then cleared his throat. "His movement had even improved, and he was talking about getting up to walk around. I went to discuss that with his doctor when the machines all went off. I knew something was wrong, and turned around. That's when I saw him having the seizure." He shook.

Jake gave him another hug. "Let's sit, Brayden." They sat in the nearest chairs. "I'm sure he's going to be okay. He has to be."

"Like Sophia?" Brayden buried his face in his palms, sobbing.

Jake felt helpless. His brother was usually strong—the pragmatic and rational doctor. He had been the family's rock during Sophia's illness. Jake wouldn't have known how to take care of her without him. He'd been on the phone with Brayden constantly those days. Jake put his arm around him, and Brayden turned and put his head on Jake's shoulder, continuing to weep.

After Brayden calmed down, he thanked Jake. "I don't know what I'll do if Dad doesn't pull out of this. Mom…she's going to…I don't even know. What are we going to do, Jake?"

How would Jake know? He sat taller. "Let's not worry about that now. Unless…" Jake's stomach twisted. "Do you think…he's not going to make it?"

"I don't know what to think. Obviously, this is out of my area of expertise, but I've never even heard of all these symptoms together. I can't help thinking the worst."

"What would you tell your patients? You know, if it wasn't your own family in this situation."

"The truth, but I always offer hope. They deserve that much."

"Well, then we need to stay hopeful. What did the doctors tell you about this?"

Brayden shook his head. "To get out of the room."

They sat in silence. Jake looked around the room. Aunts and uncles surrounded his mom. His brothers and cousins huddled in small groups. Some looked as miserable as he and Brayden, while others joked around, obviously trying to get his dad's condition out of their minds.

"How did you do it?" Brayden asked.

Jake turned to him. "Do what?"

"When Sophia was sick. You knew she was dying. How did you manage taking care of her?"

"She's my sister." Jake shrugged. "I wanted to be there for her."

"We all did, but you were the only one who dropped everything. Most of us couldn't face reality. I could hardly look at her." Brayden looked ashamed, and his voice cracked. "I'm the big time doctor, but I couldn't even come back home to help out my only sister."

Jake put his hand on Brayden's arm. "Sophia and I were always especially close. I guess because we were the babies of the family. She'd always been there for me, so I had to be there for her. I knew I wouldn't have years and years to…." Tears filled his eyes. "Well, I had to give a lifetime of support in what little time she had left. So I did."

"I wish I would have, too. I live with the regret. That's why I rushed over here when Dad was admitted." He leaned closer to Jake and whispered, "I'm speaking with my boss about transferring here. There isn't an immediate opening, but I've already spoke with the cardiology department here."

Jake's eyes widened. "You're going to leave your practice? You've spent years building that up. Plus, wouldn't working here be a pay cut?"

"A pretty significant one, but family is more important. You'd think that Sophia's death would've shown me that, but it didn't. Now I see it, though. Besides, I'm going to want to settle down and have a family at some point. I can't do that with my schedule. I sleep and work. There's no time for anything else. I want the kind of love Mom and Dad have, and that comes from actually spending time together."

"It'll be good to have you back," Jake said. "And I know Mom and Dad will be over the moon with joy."

Brayden looked away. "Hopefully Dad will recover so I can tell him the news."

"He will, Brayden. He will."

Twenty-Four

~

TIFFANY'S HEAD SPUN AS SHE stepped off the plane at Sea-Tac airport. She'd been so worried about getting back, she hadn't even thought about what she would do when she got there. Should she get on a shuttle or hail a taxi? There were always car rentals.

She should have done something to disguise herself. What if she ran into Trent or one of his friends? He probably had everyone he knew looking for her. Her chest tightened around her, constricting her breathing.

"There she is," came a voice from behind.

Tiffany's heart nearly stopped. She turned around and saw Vinny. Her legs went limp with relief.

"Are you okay?" he asked, taking her arm and steading her.

She nodded. "Just tired. Thanks for setting the flights up for me."

"Anything for you, dear. Now, let's get you to your grandpa. He's in a coma, but several of us have been stopping by and talking with him. They say hearing familiar voices will help, so you need to talk to him. Think you're up for that?"

"I'll have to be. What if something happens to him? Then I'll be left with no one."

Vinny shook his head. "Not true. Me and the other guys will take care of you. Just like he would do for our families."

Tiffany nodded. "Thanks."

"I'm sure you know we're more than just poker buddies."

"Yeah, I know."

He smiled and ruffled her hair. "Do you have a hat or something? You can't just walk around town looking like yourself. There's a reason you hightailed it out of this place."

"I don't have anything. I'll have to—"

"No. I have a hat for you." Vinny pulled out a pink Seahawks hat. "You can keep it. It's not my color, anyway."

Tiffany laughed. "I think it would bring out your eyes."

Vinny batted his eyelashes. "You think so?" He stuck the hat on her head.

"Thanks." She moved it around her hair until it was comfortable.

"Pull it down a bit. You want to cover your face some more."

Tiffany adjusted it again as they made their way to

the parking lot. Vinny talked about all kinds of things but didn't mention Tiffany's grandpa. She wanted to ask more questions, but feared the answers at the same time. If he was in a coma, it had to be really bad. She needed more information.

Trent had to be behind it. It was the only explanation. If that was the case, then she would have a good enough reason to press charges and hopefully get him put away. He couldn't be jailed for calling her names or throwing stuff at her, but putting her grandpa in the hospital—that was something he could be arrested for.

When they climbed into Vinny's car, Tiffany could only think of one way to describe it—pimped out. When he started it, she expected the wheels to jump up and down, but they didn't. He put the station on oldies, and Leslie Gore sang about crying at her party.

Tiffany looked out the window and felt strangely nostalgic. Though she hadn't been gone long, she hadn't been sure if she would ever return to the city she loved. Yet here she was already. Vinny rambled on about last night's Mariner's win as if he'd been in the dugout himself—maybe he had. She wasn't going to ask.

They made it to the hospital, and her heart sank. "They sent him to Harborview? Don't they only send the worst cases here?"

Vinny pulled into a tight spot between two SUVs, both in compact parking. "They don't only send the worst ones here, but yeah that's why he's here." He turned and faced her. "You'll want to prepare yourself, dear. He doesn't look good. He has all kinds of tubes hooked up to him, and he's not going to respond to you."

Tiffany's voice caught, so she just nodded.

"Remember what I said about talking to him? A bunch of us have spent time talking to him, but I think it'll do him a world of good to hear your voice. He's going to pull out of this, and knowing you're there is going to make a big difference, kid." Vinny squeezed her shoulder. "Let's go."

She cleared her throat. "Okay." Her head spun as they walked through the parking lot and down the halls of the hospital. She heard crying at several points walking through the hallways. Tiffany had a feeling she'd join the wailing soon enough.

"We're almost there." Vinny put his arm around her.

It felt like they were going through a maze. Tiffany was sure she wouldn't be able to get outside by herself. Her breathing was growing shallower the farther they went.

"This is the unit." Vinny removed his arm, and Tiffany looked up. The words *Critical Care* were on the wall. That sounded serious. A lump formed in her throat.

Vinny stopped where a nurse stood and spoke with her. Tiffany couldn't focus on what was said. They followed her down more halls, passing more nurses.

The hairs on the back of her neck stood up. She felt like she was being watched. Tiffany looked around but didn't see anyone looking at her. People were everywhere, but no one paid any attention to her.

Still, chills ran along her back. She turned around and looked again but couldn't see anyone who looked out of place. She decided to ignore the feelings. This wasn't the time to get suspicious. She needed to focus on Grandpa.

Finally, they entered a patient room, but all Tiffany could see was a large curtain. The nurse pulled on it, and in one swift movement, it slid to the wall.

Tiffany gasped at the sight of her grandpa lying on the bed with tubes everywhere. She ran to his side, looking at him from head to toe. "Why's he tied down? He's no criminal."

"It's for his safety," the nurse assured her. "If he thrashed around, he could hurt himself worse than he already is."

Tiffany nodded. It made sense, but it didn't mean she liked it. She rubbed his arm, and brought her face to his ear. "Grandpa, it's Tiffany. I'm here. You have to wake up. I need you." Tears filled her eyes, and she told him they would get him out of there, but he had to fight.

When she finished talking, she turned around. Vinny sat and texted, and the nurse typed on a computer.

"How long will he be in the coma?" Tiffany asked.

Still typing, the nurse said, "It's medically induced because we want to prevent any further brain damage. Did you notice how cold he is? The cooling is to give his brain the best chance possible."

"Brain damage?" Tiffany whispered.

"You can see the cuts and bruises all over his head and face. The MRI results were inconclusive, so it's a matter of being better safe than sorry."

"Is he going to be okay?"

"Of course he is," Vinny said before the nurse could respond. "Keep talking to him. Give that man a reason to sit up and order the nurses to release him."

Tiffany turned back to her grandpa, her throat nearly closing. She ran her hand along his face and whispered in his ear, telling him how much she needed him to wake up. She did her best to keep her voice steady and sound cheerful. Eventually, her voice cracked and she knew she couldn't keep up the facade anymore.

Tiffany held his hand and leaned against his arm, sobbing. Seeing him like that made it hard to imagine him ever returning to normal. What if he never came out of the coma? Or what if he couldn't take care of himself any longer?

She heard footsteps around the room, but couldn't bring herself to look up. It was probably just more nurses.

Someone asked who she was, and another person

said, "The only granddaughter."

Tiffany squeezed his hand and tried to control her sobs. More shuffling of feet. She shook, afraid she was going to lose it right there in front of all the nurses and Vinny. Maybe it didn't matter.

She felt a hand on her back. Assuming it to be Vinny, she continued crying until there was nothing left. He handed her a tissue. When she was done blowing her nose, Tiffany looked around the room. Aside from Grandpa, she was alone. She looked around, confused. She stood up and threw the tissue away.

Vinny walked in. "Sorry. The head nurse had a couple questions, and it took me longer than I thought."

Tiffany's eyebrows came together. "Wait. You weren't just here?"

He looked concerned. "No. Is everything okay?"

Blood drained from her face. Who had put his hand on her back and handed her the tissue? She tried to speak, but no words came.

"You look like you've seen a ghost."

The hairs on the back of her neck stood up again. She whipped around and stared out the door, not seeing anyone unusual. She grabbed the curtain and closed it.

"Do you need some rest, Tiff?" Vinny asked. "We can come back later."

Tiffany sat in the nearest chair. "I don't even have a place to stay."

"Of course you do. In my guest room. In fact,

Luisa's been talking nonstop about you staying with us. It's been years since we've spent any time with you, and she wants to catch up."

Tiffany nodded, unable to shake the feeling of being watched. "How safe is Grandpa here?"

"Couldn't be safer, really. Nurses come and go, checking this and that every few minutes."

Tiffany looked back at Grandpa. "I don't want to leave him, but I feel like I'm going to pass out."

"You know he wouldn't want that." Vinny texted someone. "I just told Luisa to get some food ready. We'll feed you, and then you can get some rest."

"Thank you, Vinny." Tiffany went back to Grandpa's side and ran her hands over shaved head, trying not to look at the stitches. "I'll be back, Grandpa. I'm staying in town as long as I need to. Rest up." Tears blurred her vision. "Vinny's going to take care of me. I love you." She kissed his forehead, and then turned around. "I'm ready."

As they walked through the halls, she couldn't shake the feeling of being watched. She stood as close to Vinny as she could without being weird. He must have sensed her anxiety because he put his arm around her and spoke about her grandpa's strength and iron will.

The drive home went by in a blur. Tiffany couldn't focus on anything except the image of her grandpa and all the tubes. There had even been one in his mouth, forcing him to breathe. He wouldn't have liked any of that, but it was as if any of them could do anything about it. All of that stuff kept him alive.

"Do you think Trent did that to him?" Tiffany asked, even though she was pretty sure it was him.

"No one knows, but we'll find whoever it was and put him away for life. And if the cops won't take care of it, someone else will. I promise you that much."

"Thanks, Vinny."

"The good news is that he's going to wake up, so he might be able to tell us."

"Might? Why wouldn't he?"

"The nurses and doctors are pretty sure he won't remember the event itself. I have more faith in him than that, though."

"Me, too," Tiffany said. She wasn't sure if she believed it, but she had no other choice. She had to have faith for Grandpa's sake.

Twenty-Five

~

JAKE'S PHONE WOKE HIM. HE rolled over in bed trying to find it. It was twisted up in the sheets.

"Cruz? What's going on?" he asked into the phone. His voice sounded like a frog.

"I need some sleep, man. It's time for you to take over the shop."

Jake groaned. "At some point, I'm going to need to sleep for three days straight. I can't keep this up. Can't Rafael work the till for a while?"

Cruz laughed. "You're kidding, right? The Hunter Family Shop is beneath him."

"Right. He's probably counting the minutes until he gets back to LA so he can direct some bigwig fashion show." Jake closed his eyes, hoping to fall back to sleep.

No such luck.

"Dude, tell me about it. But at least there's help now."

Jake squeezed a blanket. "Oh, right. You hired those kids. How'd the first one do?"

"She was great. Fast learner."

"Okay. Can you wait for me to at least get a shower and some coffee? Strong coffee."

Cruz yawned on the other end of the phone. "Do whatever you need to. Just don't take your time. I'm about to fall over, and I'd prefer that to happen in my old bed."

"Yeah, I'll hurry." Jake got off the phone and into the shower, but first he set up the coffee maker. Despite his promise to hurry, he stood unmoving as the hot water ran over him. It massaged his aching muscles but couldn't reach his frayed nerves.

When the water cooled, he rinsed off and got out. When he stood near the door, he could smell the coffee. It made his mouth water, and he perked up a bit. After dressing and brushing his hair, he went into the kitchen and pulled out a couple travel mugs. He prepared coffee for both him and Cruz. It was the least he could do after taking so much time in the shower.

His stomach rumbled, but he could grab a bite to eat at the shop. It was a convenience store, after all. Jake balanced the two cups and locked the house up before hurrying to the shop.

"Took you long enough." Cruz gave him an irritated look.

Jake shoved a coffee in his face. "Peace offering. Even though I got some sleep, I'm still exhausted. Sue me."

"Thanks." Cruz took the cup and sipped. "Mmm. This is good. You've gotten better at making coffee."

"It was *one time,*" Jake said. "I'm never going to hear the end of it, am I?"

"Nope." Cruz took another long sip. "I'll never know how you managed to burn coffee."

"Go home." Jake waved toward the door. "Wait. Any news on Dad?"

"Oh, yeah. Thanks for reminding me. I almost forgot to tell you. The short story is they've got him on medications for the seizures and he's doing a lot better. He's back to wanting to walk around again, but they want to keep a close eye on him."

"He's probably going to get up as soon as the doctors turn around."

"No probably about it." Cruz went around the counter. "I'll leave my phone on, but only call me if there's an emergency. I need some sleep. Oh, and if you want to go to the hospital later, I'll leave my keys on the kitchen counter. I'm not going back today. I gotta sleep."

"I can take Mom and Dad's car."

Cruz shook his head. "Brayden has it."

Jake rolled his eyes. "He would. I wasn't even aware he'd been to the house."

"You know how it goes. See ya." Cruz turned around and headed for the door.

"Bye." Jake went around to the register and looked

through it. Cruz had made a mess of it, but Jake couldn't complain. At least Cruz was helping. That was more than he could say for any of his other relatives.

A group of kids headed for the counter. Jake took a swig of coffee and prepared himself for a long afternoon. He hoped Elena would stop by. He really missed her. Had she already stopped by? Cruz would have mentioned it, wouldn't he?

After the lunch rush died down, a kid in a powder-blue polo shirt and khaki shorts walked in, heading straight for the counter.

"Can I help you?" Jake asked.

"I'm Calvin."

Jake raised an eyebrow. Customers didn't usually introduce themselves. "Jake."

"Right. Cruz mentioned a brother. What do you want me to do?"

"Do?"

The kid looked deflated. "I'm supposed to work here." It sounded more like a question than a statement.

"Oh. Right." Jake looked at him again. He didn't even look old enough to drive, but maybe he would helpful around the shop. "Sorry. It's been a really long week."

"That's what Cruz said. How's your dad?"

"He appears to be turning around. Thanks for asking. Have you worked in a convenience store before?"

Calvin shook his head. "My parents bought a summer home here, and I'm bored out of my mind already. I figure I may as well do something useful and build my resume."

"Okay. Let's start by learning how to use this thing." Jake slapped the register. "The afternoon rush is going to slam us soon, and if we can both check people out, it's going to make life easier on everyone."

Calvin was a fast learner, and even quicker getting customers checked out. He appeared to enjoy himself. Before Jake knew it, the kid's shift was over, and Jake was back to manning the shop himself. Only then did he realize that he still hadn't seen Elena.

There was a lull, so he walked around the shelves picking up items that had been knocked over and put back in the wrong places by hungry customers. Another rush hit—why couldn't they ever just trickle in?—and then Jake closed up shop. It was a little early, but they had made more money with the two new employees.

He locked the shop and then held his head and twisted it, stretching the sore, tired muscles in his neck.

"You okay, Jake?"

Jake turned around to look at Dimitri. "Yeah. Just tired of being tired, you know? I wish life would calm down for a bit. I can't catch a break."

"At least you have a pretty lady." Dimitri smiled wide, showing some gold teeth near the back. "She really likes you."

Jake couldn't help doubting. He hadn't even had a

text from her all day. What if pouring his heart out had pushed her away? They'd connected, but then maybe his brokenness had scared her. She probably wanted someone stronger—she must think he was weak. There was a reason the girls always wanted his brothers over him.

"Are you okay?" asked Dimitri.

"Yeah." Jake shook his head to clear it. "I need to take a walk, and think."

"That'll do you good." Dimitri nodded knowingly. "Then take the girl for dessert."

"I'll do that." Jake walked away, lost in thought. He went over every detail of the time spent with Elena on the beach. She hadn't seemed upset or put off by anything, at least that he could remember. He shrugged and decided not to worry about it. She had enough going on in her own life, and she was probably busy with something that had nothing to do with him.

He stopped at a crosswalk and realized he was in front of Bobby's auto shop. Had he gone there on purpose? Either way, it would be helpful to find out what Bobby knew. He went inside and looked at tires until Bobby's line died down.

"Hey, dude." Bobby held out his fist.

Jake bumped it. "How's it going?"

"Busy as always. I think this is the year I'm finally going to add that extension to my house."

"Awesome. You'll have to have me over."

"Yeah. I'm going to have a huge party."

"I wouldn't miss it. So, have you heard from Elena today?" asked Jake.

"No. I've called both her phone and her gramps'. The car was easy enough to fix, so hopefully they don't get too pissed that I fixed it without his approval. I was supposed to talk to the old man before touching it." Bobby shrugged. "It's purring like a kitten now, so they should be happy. Hope that doesn't put a damper on your plans, dude."

"We hit it off, but I don't know if I've convinced her to stay any longer."

"Then go wherever she's going."

Jake frowned. "I wish. There's so much going on right now with my family. My dad's in the hospital, and the shop won't take care of itself."

Bobby pushed Jake's shoulder. "Man, you gotta think about yourself for a change."

"Maybe."

"Dude." Bobby stared him down.

"Text me if you hear from her." Jake frowned, and turned away.

"Sow those wild oats."

Jake grunted, and then reached for the door. Wild oats? Him?

He wandered the busy streets, wondering what he could do that would be exciting. Maybe tattoos, like Bobby and Cruz. He didn't want some dragon that took up an entire leg. That had been Cruz's first one—much to their mom's horror. Jake would never forget the look on her face, or the sound of her shrill screaming. She had eventually come around and accepted the body art, but it had been a difficult time for everyone involved until she did.

Jake looked around and saw the tall hotel where Elena was staying. He didn't even know what floor she was on, but maybe he could leave her a message. Of course, he could call or text, but if he went into the hotel lobby, he actually stood a chance of seeing her.

Once inside, he went to the main desk. An older lady looked at him from above the rims of her glasses. "May I help you?"

Jake cleared his throat. "I'd like to leave a message with one of your guests."

"Sure, dear. What's her room number?"

Jake looked around, feeling gazes from strangers on him. "I'm not sure. I just have her name."

A younger lady looked at Jake from behind the counter. "Do you mean the cute brunette you were with the other evening? You two make the cutest couple. Where'd she go to in such a hurry?"

Jake's heart sank. "When?"

The two women exchanged a look.

"You mean you don't know?" asked the younger one.

"Apparently not." Jake frowned.

The younger one leaned forward, her eyes wide. "She jumped in a cab, and I swear the tires left rubber on our pavement, the way they squealed away."

Jake stared at her for a minute. "I think I'd be better off calling her. Thanks for your help." He turned around and went back outside, slouching in defeat.

When had she taken off like that? And why? At least Elena's car was still in Bobby's shop. She had to come back. Right?

Twenty-Six

~

"Tiffany. Tiffany, wake up."

She mumbled and rubbed her eyes, not wanting to open them. "What's going on?"

"They're going to wake your grandpa, honey."

Tiffany sat up and stared at Luisa, Vinny's wife. "When?"

"They called hours ago, saying that they were starting the process. He's expected to wake in about an hour or two."

"Why didn't you wake me sooner?"

Luisa kissed the top of her head. "You needed your rest. By the time you get cleaned up and I feed you, we'll have just enough time to get to the hospital to see him wake."

"They didn't say anything about waking him when we were there. I didn't even know they could do that when someone's in a coma."

"That was yesterday. Besides, didn't they tell you it was a medically-induced coma?"

Tiffany tried to remember, but her brain was still in a fog. "I don't know. Maybe."

"Well, get ready, sweetie. I'm going to make you some good food. I'll bet you haven't had any since you left, have you?"

"Nothing like your home cooking."

Luisa beamed. "Hurry, hurry. Oh, and I washed your clothes for you."

Tiffany threw her arms around the lady who was as close to a grandma as Tiffany would ever have. "Thank you."

An hour and half later, Tiffany was in the car with Vinny and Luisa. Her stomach was stuffed with delicious, authentic Italian food.

"What do you think is going to happen when he wakes?" Tiffany asked.

"I expect it won't be like the movies," Vinny said. "It would be nice if he sat up and put on his running shoes, but I imagine he'll be groggy and confused. He won't remember what happened or know why he's there."

Tiffany's heart pounded in her chest. "You don't think he'll forget us, do you?" Suddenly, she felt like a little girl. What if her only family member didn't know who she was? She wasn't sure she could survive it.

Luisa looked at Vinny. "They said the part of his brain with long-term memory was fine, didn't they?"

"Yeah. It was the part that runs motor skills they

couldn't get a good reading for."

Tears filled Tiffany's eyes. She couldn't imagine Grandpa unable to walk or feed himself. Not only that, but he would hate living like that.

Luisa looked back at Tiffany. "He's going to be fine, honey. We have to believe, and if anyone can beat his, it's our Alfy."

Tiffany nodded, afraid to speak.

Vinny turned up the music. The Byrds sang about different seasons of life. Tiffany hoped she and grandpa were about to enter a good season. She'd just left Trent—and managed not to think about him obsessively for a while—so it was time for a happy season. Grandpa needed it, too.

Before long, they parked at the hospital. Tiffany's pulse raced. As much as she hated seeing her grandpa in the coma, she was even more scared of what was to come. The unknown was a cruel beast, not even giving her the chance to prepare. Should she get herself ready for the worst, or the best? Oh, what she wouldn't give for a crystal ball to see into the future.

Luisa put her arms around Tiffany as they walked through the maze of hospital halls. Tiffany looked around. It didn't even look the same as it had the day before. Were they really in the same place? Maybe she was the one who needed to be sedated.

When they got to the critical care unit, everything looked familiar. Vinny and Luisa spoke to a nurse, and

Tiffany walked over to a large fish tank. Strange, brightly colored fish swam around without a care in the world. She wished she could trade places with one of them. At least for now. She watched a little pink fish swim around near the bottom, poking the gravel every so often.

The hair on the back of her neck stood up, and chills ran through her. Was someone watching her? She turned around, staring in every direction. There was no one in sight, aside from some people in the waiting room minding their own business. Most of them had been there the day before.

Tiffany turned back to the tank. She used the reflection from the glass to look behind her. Nothing looked out of place, but she couldn't shake the feeling of being watched. No one even resembled Trent.

Tiffany watched a bright orange fish chase a plant that moved back and forth in the water. Oh, to be a fish with no real problems.

A hand rested on her back, and Tiffany jumped. Her pulse pounded in her ears as she turned around. It was just Luisa.

"Sorry, honey. I didn't mean to startle you."

"It's not your fault. Can we go back there and see him?"

"She said that's fine. They've taken him off all the sedatives, and he's just starting to move around a little. He hasn't opened his eyes, but given his movements, they expect that any time."

"I hope he's okay."

Luisa squeezed her shoulder. "He will be. Are you ready?"

"As much as I'm ever going to be."

Vinny walked over to them. "We might get to see him wake up, Tiff. I think that'll help a lot."

Tiffany nodded, too choked up to speak. They walked to his room in silence. Despite how upset she was, Tiffany still felt like someone was watching her. Not that it would have surprised her if Trent had someone staked out in the hospital to look for her. But he wouldn't be stupid enough to approach her there. Not with doctors, nurses, and plenty of security guards.

She pushed the thought out of her mind as they approached Grandpa's room. The curtain was pulled back, and she could see him on the bed. He didn't look any different, but as she neared him, she noticed the restraints had at least been removed. He still had the breathing tube hooked to the ventilator and a maze of tubes hooked to both arms.

Holding her breath, she walked up to the bed. "Grandpa?"

He didn't respond. She put her hand on his arm. It was warmer than it had been the day before.

Vinny and Luisa went around to the other side of the bed and rubbed his other arm, talking to him.

Tiffany's vision went blurry. Would he ever wake

up? She slid her hand in his. "Grandpa, it's Tiffany. I'm here. Vinny and Luisa are, too. We really want to see you open your eyes."

A nurse stood next to her, checking his vitals. "It could be another hour or so. This isn't an exact science, and the drugs he's coming off are potent. Just be aware everyone reacts differently. We have reason to believe he'll be fine—the results didn't show anything obviously wrong. Sometimes, the readings don't come out perfectly." She gave Tiffany a sympathetic smile. "I have high expectations for your grandpa."

Tiffany cleared her throat. "Thanks." She squeezed Grandpa's hand. "Did you hear that? It's time to wake up."

The nurse typed into the computer, and then turned around, looking at Tiffany. "You guys might want to pull up chairs. It can take a while to wake up from a medically-induced coma." She left the room.

Luisa looked at Tiffany. "Do you want a chair?"

"I'll wait." She stood, talking to Grandpa for a while. He squeezed her hand every so often and moved his arms from time to time. It wasn't much, but the progress was a huge relief after seeing him not moving at all before.

She wasn't sure how much time had passed, but her legs ached. It was probably time to get a chair. She looked around for one, and then her grandpa pulled on Tiffany's arm.

Tiffany turned around in surprise. He moved his head, and she swore he tried to speak.

"Did you hear that?" she asked.

Luisa and Vinny both nodded.

"We're right here, Alfy," Vinny said. "You missed our last card game, so you gotta wake up. You can't miss the next one."

Grandpa moved around some more, but his eyes remained closed. Tiffany sighed, fighting back tears. Her grandpa was a tough, strong man. Seeing him like this just felt wrong—and it was even worse not knowing if he would ever go back to normal.

She thought back to her last conversation with him. Why hadn't she told him how much he meant to her? She had never told him how much she appreciated him raising her in his retirement years. Those were years he shouldn't have had to deal with a resentful teenager who was angry at the world because her parents weren't around.

Did he know how much she valued him? Tears spilled over and ran down her face. Would he ever know the difference he made in her life? Without him, she would have been a huge mess. Sure, she had problems and had managed to mess up her life by marrying a jerk when she was too young to know better. But without Grandpa's influence, she would have made worse, life-altering decisions in high school. She could have been in that car full of kids that crashed because they were all high. No one had survived.

Tiffany shook, and then she felt arms around her.

"He's going to be okay," Luisa whispered. "We just have to give him time."

Vinny slid a chair over, and they both helped her sit. Luisa handed her tissues. Tiffany tried to blow her nose quietly, but it was pointless because the tears wouldn't stop. Guilt squeezed her, and many what-ifs ran through her mind.

Luisa gave her the entire box of tissues, and she stayed at Tiffany's side. When Tiffany finally regained control of herself, she threw the pile into the trash, used some sanitizer, and then grabbed Grandpa's hand again. "It's time to wake up, Grandpa. We really want to talk to you. You can go back to sleep later, but we have to talk to you."

"Yeah," Vinny agreed. "We don't have time to wait around all day. We got places to go."

Tiffany cracked a smile, and Vinny winked at her.

They spoke to him for a little longer, and Vinny continued to egg on his lifelong friend. Tiffany rubbed Grandpa's bald head, and she could feel bumps all over. "Come on. Wake up and tell us what happened."

His eyes fluttered, and Tiffany gasped, jumping back. They watched, no one speaking, for several minutes until his eyes finally opened slowly. He looked around, obviously confused.

Tiffany froze. She knew she should say something,

or at least hold his hand again, but she couldn't get her body to cooperate.

Vinny put his hands on Grandpa's arm. "Alfy, you're in the hospital, old buddy. Luisa and I are here with Tiffany."

Grandpa looked around until he made eye contact with Tiffany. His eyes widened, almost looking fearful.

"It's okay, Grandpa," Tiffany said, her voice shaking. Was he scared of her? "The doctors say you're going to be fine. You just needed some rest." She tried to sound more reassuring than she felt.

He shook his head, and then tried to say something, but the ventilator made it impossible to understand.

"Relax, Alfy," Vinny said. "You're going to hurt yourself."

Grandpa moved his hands up toward his face slowly, and pulled on the mask.

Luisa and Vinny both grabbed his arms. "Take it easy, Alfy," Luisa said. "You don't need to speak yet."

He shook his head, looking frantic. Again, he appeared to try to talk, but no words came. He fought to get free from Vinny and Luisa's grips.

Vinny looked at Tiffany. "Go get a nurse. Now."

Tiffany ran to the door. "Nurse!" She looked around. The hall was empty—no one was even at the nurse's station. She could hear beeping and frantic conversation in a nearby room. She ran down the hall, calling for a nurse.

A man about her age stepped out from the waiting room. They made eye contact, and Tiffany froze. He looked familiar, but she couldn't place him. He continued to stare at her but didn't say anything.

He twitched, and for some reason, she realized where she knew him.

"You're Trent's cousin. Josh, isn't it?"

Josh turned around.

"Wait."

He stopped—much to Tiffany's disbelief.

"Are you the one who's been watching me? Did you give me the tissue?"

He backed up a couple steps.

"Where's Trent?"

Josh ran down the hall. Tiffany almost ran after him but remembered why she was in the hall. She turned around and looked in an open door. A doctor sat at a computer. "We need help," she said. "My grandpa just woke up, and he's struggling to—"

The doctor stood up. "Take me to him. Where are the nurses?" He looked down that hall, irritation covering his face.

Tiffany led him to the room. Grandpa was still fighting against Vinny and Luisa.

The doctor went over to the bed and took one of Grandpa's hands. "I need you to calm down, sir. I'm a doctor, and I can help. If you relax, we'll be able to listen to what you have to say. Do you understand what

I'm saying?"

Grandpa stopped struggling and nodded. He remained still and continued to look at the doctor.

"Thank you, sir," the doctor said. "Your nurse and doctor are both busy with another patient at the moment. I'm going to have your friends here explain your situation to me." He turned to Vinny. "Can you tell me about your friend?"

Vinny gave a brief summarization while the doctor nodded and asked a few questions.

He turned back to Grandpa. "Waking up in a hospital can be most scary. I've actually had that happen, too. It—"

Grandpa shook his head and pointed to the device in his mouth.

"It's too soon to take that out." He looked at one of the machines Grandpa was hooked up to. "Your oxygen levels do look good. We might be able to take this out shortly, after having some time to observe you in your awake state."

Grandpa shook his head again.

"Is there something you want to tell us?" Luisa asked.

Grandpa nodded, eyes wide.

Luisa looked at the doctor. "Can we let him write it down?"

"Sure. I've got a pad of paper here." The doctor dug into his lab coat and pulled it out. He helped Grandpa with the pad and a pen.

Grandpa's eyes narrowed as he wrote. When he was done, he shoved the paper toward Vinny.

Vinny's eyes widened, and then he handed the pad to Tiffany.

She took it. Grandpa's handwriting was messier than normal, but every word was legible:

Get Tiffany out of here now.

Twenty-Seven

~

JAKE LEANED AGAINST THE BUILDING outside the shop and took a deep breath, trying to let the sun's warm rays dissolve his stress. It had been a horrible morning. Most of the customers had been angry about something. Thankfully, Bella was a cheerful employee, and she handled each person with a level of grace and kindness that Jake never could have.

Some of the people had been so rude to her, he wanted to deck them. Yet she held her sunny disposition, and found ways for everyone to leave with a smile on their faces—or at least without the scowl they had come in wearing.

Jake pulled out his phone. He'd missed a call from his mom. Still no calls or texts from Elena. He couldn't stop worrying. Something had to be wrong, or she wouldn't ignore his calls and texts.

Had he done something to scare her off? They'd hit it off so well, but he had a tendency to say the wrong things to girls, especially when he wanted to impress them.

If Elena wanted nothing to do with him, he would accept that, but he just wanted to know. Of course, he wanted to try to fix anything he had done wrong, but not knowing ate away at him.

Then there was the thought of her ex. She was clearly scared of him. What if he had found her? Could that have been why she took off in such a hurry? What if her ex had forced her into the cab?

Was she okay? They'd hit it off so well, that seemed to be the most likely scenario. She'd been so happy with him when they had parted ways.

Jake let out a slow breath. He had no proof that she was in danger. The girl at the hotel didn't say anything about Elena going into the cab with anyone. Or about her looking scared.

"Are you okay, my friend?"

Jake jumped, and then looked over to see Dimitri headed his way. He shrugged, hoping his friend would take the hint.

"How are your new employees working out?" Dimitri leaned against the building next to Jake, oblivious to Jake's mood.

Jake grunted.

"Must be nice to finally have some help, huh?"

Jake took a deep breath, and then glared at Dimitri.

"Why don't you look happy?"

"Because everything sucks."

Dimitri raised an eyebrow.

Jake stared at him, almost daring him to keep talking.

"Ah." Dimitri nodded knowingly. "You still haven't heard back from Elena?"

Jake shook his head.

Dimitri patted his shoulder. "I saw the way she looked at you. She'll call."

Jake tried to give his friend a dirty look, but couldn't even do that right.

"Hope is not lost, my friend. Even if the pretty lady doesn't return, you can find her. Everyone's on social media. Pick a site, and we'll search every Elena until we find her. If she's not there, we'll try another one." He pulled out a tablet. "Where do you want to start?"

"If she won't answer my calls, what makes you think she's going to friend me online?"

Dimitri looked into Jake's eyes, and then squeezed Jake's cheeks. "Because no one can resist that face." He burst out laughing. "Seriously, Jake, she has the look of love. Something came up, and she's just busy. You know, like all this stuff with your dad. You're hard to get a hold of, and you haven't spent much time with your friends. I should know."

Jake ran his fingers through his hair. "Sorry. Yeah, I guess you're right."

"Of course I am. Want to grab a drink with lunch? Dimitri's treat."

"I don't know...I'm on the clock."

"And you need a lunch break."

Jake looked at his cell phone. "Bella's shift is almost over."

"And she can see how stressed you are. She won't mind staying a few extra minutes."

"I can't."

"You're a lost cause." Dimitri walked past Jake and went in the shop. Less than a minute later, he was back out. "She's more than happy to help you out. Come on, pal. We're getting lunch."

Dimitri dragged Jake to a nearby bar that served mouth-watering appetizers. Once seated, Dimitri ordered drinks and their largest snack platter. Five people could eat from it and still have leftovers. He spoke about some of the town gossip while they waited.

Jake nodded, but he could tell Dimitri knew he was barely listening. When the beers arrived, Jake drank his like it was water. The alcohol relaxed him, and he finally joined his friend in the conversation.

Soon, they were laughing about the antics their old schoolmates had pulled back in the day. By the time they left the bar, Jake was not only relaxed and happy, but he was full, and ready to tackle the afternoon shift.

When they got back to the shop, Dimitri gave him a good-natured whack on the back. "Glad to see you smiling again. You remember this next time you see Dimitri down."

"Will do. Thanks, buddy." Jake punched his arm lightly. "We have to do that again soon." He went inside and thanked Bella for staying late.

"No problem. I hope people are nicer to you this afternoon."

Jake leaned against the counter. "I can handle them, either way."

"Oh," Bella said, gathering her things, "some girl came in looking for you."

"What? Who?"

"A pretty brunette with green eyes and freckles. What did she say her name was…?"

"Elena?"

Bella's eyes lit up. "Yeah. Elena. Like, from the *Vampire Diaries*. I told her you were out for lunch. I'm sure she'll be back. She looked pretty anxious."

"What do you mean? In a good or bad way?"

She scrunched her face, looking deep in thought. "Like…well, she kept looking over her shoulder. It was weird. I asked her if she was okay, but she said yeah."

Jake looked around. "Do you know where she went?"

"No. She didn't say. You want me to stay longer so you can find her?"

"I don't want to do that to you. You've been here long enough."

"Doesn't bother me. I can't wait to get my first check to have spending money. The more I work, the more I can buy." She smiled.

Jake looked up at the clock. "I don't want to break any labor laws. I don't know how many hours we can even let you work in a day."

Bella pulled out a phone. "I'll look it up."

"No, no, no. You need to get some lunch. Calvin will be here in a few. If I need to find Elena, I'll just wait for him."

"Your call." Bella put the cell phone back in her pocket. "See ya tomorrow, boss." She went to the back room, and came out with a beach bag, waving as she left.

Jake went around to the register and sat down. The next few customers he rang up were all pleasant and happy. Maybe the town's grumpiness had subsided. Calvin arrived after a couple rounds of ringing up items. No sooner did he arrive than the afternoon rush hit. The next time Jake looked at the time, nearly three and a half hours had passed.

Calvin gave him a high-five. "We handled that like pros. I've never seen it so busy."

"Some days it gets worse."

"Really?" Calvin asked.

"Yeah, like on the weekends. Saturday mornings can be terrible with half the people leaving and others coming in for the next week. Sometimes Friday evenings are just as bad."

"Awesome. Can I work Saturday?"

Jake arched an eyebrow. "You want to work on Saturday?"

"Yeah. This is so cool."

Jake held back a laugh. Give the kid a few weeks, and he'd be moaning about Mondays soon enough. "If you want. I really need to look into child labor laws."

"I'm no child." Calvin frowned.

"You're a minor, and I know there are strict laws about how many hours you can work."

"I don't care. When's the lull over? I'm already getting bored."

"Really? We have some boxes in the back room that need to be stocked on the shelves."

"Cool. Thanks." He headed in that direction.

Jake chuckled. To be young and that excited about working. He looked out the window and saw a band playing on the beach. A large crowd gathered around. Hopefully, that meant things would be quiet for a while.

He grabbed his phone and scrolled to Elena's number. His finger hovered over the call button. He'd already called several times, but that was before she'd stopped by looking for him. She might actually answer this time.

Jake moved his finger down, but then stopped just before touching the screen. She hadn't called him. Maybe she didn't want him to call. Or maybe she was waiting for him to call first. He tapped the button before he could further talk himself out of it.

It rang three times. He debated whether or not to leave a message.

"Jake?"

He nearly dropped the phone. She had actually answered. "Elena? Is everything okay? I've been trying to get a hold of you."

"I know. I'm sorry. A lot has happened in the last few days."

"Are you all right? You sound upset."

She breathed heavily into the phone. "I can't explain it now. When do you get off work?"

"As soon as you need me. I can call one of my brothers and have them take over." Jake had given Cruz the day off, but if Elena needed him, he would drag Cruz away from whatever he was doing.

"Okay. Can you meet me at that beach where we chased each other?"

"No problem. I can be there in an hour. Maybe sooner if Cruz is ready."

"Thanks, Jake."

The call ended.

Twenty-Eight

~

TIFFANY LOOKED AROUND FROM THE tree. She couldn't see Trent, but that didn't mean anything. He could be nearby. Her pulse raced, rushing in her ears. When she'd arrived in the small airport and thought she saw Trent, she had to do a double-take. How would he know to find her there? As it turned out, it had been some other guy.

Then after the taxi dropped her off at Bobby's auto shop, Tiffany thought she saw him again. Just like before, it was someone else. She was half-tempted to jump in her car and drive as far away as she could, but she had to see Jake one last time.

Trent wouldn't actually be in Kittle Falls. He was still in Seattle. That was why her grandpa had been so eager to get her out of there. He wouldn't calm down until Vinny booked Tiffany's flight out.

She barely had time to give Grandpa a tearful good-bye before Luisa drove her to the airport. Ever since leaving the hospital, Tiffany couldn't shake the feeling of being watched. The hairs on the back of her neck would fall off soon from all the raising. She had probably been imagining it, but she *hadn't* imagined running into Josh.

When she arrived in town, Tiffany found a cheap, rundown motel on the outskirts of town. If Trent did follow her, she wasn't going to stay in the same hotel as before. What if he already knew her new identity? He could know where she'd been staying—and where her car was.

Tiffany hoped that hiding out in the smelly motel had been enough to throw Trent off her trail. She couldn't take anymore, and finally checked out. She couldn't see anyone suspicious, but then again what did she know? If someone was spying on her, they would be smart enough to blend in.

She took a deep breath and went around the tree. No one appeared to pay any attention to her—not that she could see, anyway. She stayed as close to the beach as she could, away from the crowd. There were still a lot of people near the beach, and this area was less busy than the main part of town.

The hairs on the back of her neck rose again, but she was so used to it, she didn't even slow down. Tiffany continued on her way, this time standing near a group of people. She tiptoed around them, and then jumped to the nearest crowd, pretending to be part of it.

Tiffany kept that up for about fifteen minutes until

she was sure, or at least hopeful, that she'd lost whoever might have been following her. She walked away from the crowd and headed for the non-touristy part of town. Relief swept over her the farther she got from the crowds.

She kept looking back. No one stood out. Everyone appeared to be a part of something going on at the beach. She made a split-second decision to run. It may have been dumb, but she didn't care. The sneaking around made her crazy.

Jake would be waiting for her, and she just wanted to see him. Tiffany would tell him everything—fill in the details she had left out before. Things like Elena not being her real name. He deserved the truth, even if he never wanted to see her again.

Her heart constricted at the thought.

Part of her—okay, most of her—hoped he'd suggest they run off together. But with his dad in the hospital, she knew how unlikely that was. Tiffany hadn't wanted to leave Grandpa, and the only reason she had was because he had insisted that she was in danger. She couldn't ask Jake to leave his family—or put himself in harm's way. Trent was dangerous, and Jake didn't deserve to deal with him.

All of a sudden, she regretted refusing to learn how to use a gun. Grandpa had offered to teach her, but Tiffany was sure it wouldn't do any good. She'd heard that most victims had their guns used on them. Why give anyone that much power over her?

The secret beach finally came into sight. Tiffany picked up her speed, and pushed through her fatigue. She was not only physically tired from traveling—and the bed in the motel was lumpy and it smelled weird—but she was also emotionally exhausted.

Tiffany had to push through. Going back to Seattle had probably only served to alert Trent to her new location. Though they were careful with the flight reservations, it would likely take little digging to figure out where she had gone. She had taken on her grandma's name, after all.

She scanned the beach, finding it empty. Movement from the far end caught her attention. At first, she thought it was seagulls flying around, but then she squinted her eyes and put her hand over her face to block then sun. It was Jake.

Tiffany felt simultaneously relieved and energized. She picked up her pace, and ran toward him. He appeared to see her, too, and raced also.

When she reached him, they rushed into each other's arms. Jake held her tightly, and she returned the squeeze. She never wanted to let go. She finally felt safe again. Her anxiety melted away in his arms. Everything was going to be okay. She didn't know how, but it would.

"What happened?" he whispered into her ear. "Where were you?"

"My grandpa was injured. He doesn't remember what happened, but I think Trent did it. Grandpa had been researching him, and somehow Trent must have found out. I don't really know anything, but he wouldn't let me stay there. Grandpa wanted me back here so he could know I was safe. I kept feeling like someone was watching me." Tiffany shivered.

Jake held her closer. "Are you safe here? Do you think he followed you?"

Tiffany rested her face on his shoulder. "I don't know."

"Would he hurt you?"

"I'm sure of it."

He looked her in the eyes. "We've got to do something. You really don't know if you're being followed?"

"I felt like I was being watched, but I haven't seen him."

Jake frowned. "Maybe we should go to the police."

"And tell them what? That the hairs on my neck won't stay down? We have no proof."

"We could print out his picture and put it all over town. Say he's wanted and dangerous. Then everyone would be on the lookout for him."

Tiffany thought about it. "What I need is a new car. He might know what I'm driving since he's been watching my grandpa. Do you think Bobby would trade a car with me?"

Pain covered Jake's face. "I can't let you leave on

your own. I'm going with you."

Her eyes widened. "Are you sure? What about your dad? Isn't he still—?"

"All my other relatives are here. No one's going to miss me. They'll understand."

"But you—"

"You're not going to talk me out of this, Elena. I can't send you away on your own."

Tiffany felt tears threatening. "Thank you."

"First, we need to—" Jake stopped, staring at something behind her.

"What?" asked Tiffany.

"What does Trent look like?"

Tiffany turned around, and then gasped. She saw the tall, stocky figure in the distance. "No!"

"It's him?"

She turned back to Jake, knowing the look of dread in her face answered his question. Jake grabbed her hand, and ran in the opposite direction of Trent.

Tiffany's feet stumbled in the sand, but she managed to get control of her footing, and kept up with Jake. She turned her head back, and saw Trent running after them. Her heart sank, but what else should she have expected? For him to turn around in defeat because they ran away? He'd followed her all the way from Washington to California. He wasn't going to give up without a fight.

She felt light-headed at the thought. Would she

have to actually fight him?

Fear shot through her, but it was quickly replaced with anger. How dare Trent hurt someone Tiffany loved with all her heart? Was he jealous that he would never be half the man her grandpa was?

Tiffany's ankle twisted underneath her, and she stumbled. Her knees hit the ground, sending sand in all directions.

Jake stopped, and helped her up. When Tiffany stood, sharp pain shot out from her ankle. She cried out.

"You can't walk?" Jake asked, looking behind her.

She shook her head. "I hurt my ankle. Just go. I'll deal with Trent."

"Are you kidding? I'm not leaving you here."

"I can't let him hurt you like he did my grandpa."

Jake looked disgusted. He reached down and scooped her up.

"I'm only going to slow you down," Tiffany said.

"When he catches up, I'll fight him off while you escape. Find a large piece of driftwood and use it for a crutch if you have to. Just get away."

"Okay." Tiffany had no intention of running off while Jake, who hadn't done anything to Trent, fought him off. She wasn't going to tell him that, though. He would just insist she get away.

Trent moved faster than them, closing the distance with each step.

Tiffany looked on the ground for anything that

could be used as a weapon. Like Jake mentioned, there was plenty of driftwood. She could hit Trent over the head with a piece, but it wouldn't do much considering he had such a thick head. She could throw sand in his face. That would buy a little time. Not much, though. It was something at least.

What else was there? There were trees, but if she climbed one, Trent could also, and with more ease since Tiffany hurt her ankle. There were seashells closer to the water. Many were broken. Perhaps she could cut him with one. Were there any jellyfish in the water? She would love sticking some down his shorts to sting him where the sun doesn't shine.

With a little creativity, she and Jake would have no problem getting away from Trent. There were two of them and only one of him.

Trent was now close enough that Tiffany could hear the sand crunching under his feet.

"Stop," Trent demanded.

Jake kept going. Tiffany made the mistake of making eye contact with Trent. The look on his face was enough to make her stomach drop. She'd never seen him so angry—and that said something.

Trent's lips were pursed together, his eyebrows furrowed, and the look in his eyes was pure fury. His eyes narrowed as he stared at her. He reached for her, but was too far away. It was only a matter of minutes—if that—before he was close enough to reach them.

"Hurry," Tiffany whispered in Jake's ear.

"I'm doing my best."

"I know."

Trent reached out again, and this time his fingernails brushed against Tiffany's elbow. She let out a scream.

Jake sped up, but so did Trent. He grabbed a handful of Tiffany's hair, yanking her toward him. She could feel Jake stumble. Tiffany wrapped her hands around Trent's, trying to free her hair. He pulled on her with his other hand, and somehow the three of them all fell to the ground. Jake's grip on her loosened, and Tiffany bounced across the ground, getting sand in her mouth and eyes.

She wiped the sand away from her face, and spit out the pieces in her mouth.

Trent grabbed Jake with one arm, and held his other fist up. "You'd better get out of here before I damage your pretty face, you stupid, little wimp."

"Wimp?" Jake asked, shoving Trent. "You pick on women and old men. Are you afraid to go after someone your own size?"

"Shut up. Did you know the woman you're with is married? No one would pity you if I beat the crap out of you. You're nothing other than a home-wrecker."

Jake shook his head. "You're something else. You're an abuser—nobody's going to feel sorry for *you*. In fact, when you go to jail for what you did to Elena and her grandpa, you're going to become someone's b—"

"Elena?" Trent asked, and then laughed. "Is that what she said her name is?"

Tiffany's stomach twisted in knots, and she felt like her lunch was going to come up.

Jake looked over at her, his face full of confusion and hurt.

Twenty-Nine

~

JAKE LOOKED BACK AND FORTH between Elena and Trent. Her eyes were wide and pleading.

"Didn't see that coming, did you?" Trent laughed. "I wonder what else she lied to you about. Makes you doubt what she told you about me, doesn't it?"

It hurt that he didn't know Elena's real name, but then again, she had told him that she was on the run. She probably had to start over with an entirely new identity to get away from the jerk grabbing his arm.

Jake turned and glared at Trent, moving out of his grip. "Actually, no. Elena is her new name. She doesn't want her old one because it's associated with you, and all the pain you caused her."

Trent rolled his eyes. "Isn't that cute? You believe her lies—and that's all they are. She has mental issues. You're aware of that, aren't you?" His spit landed on Jake's face.

Jake wiped it off, not taking his eyes off Trent. "I find that hard to believe, given that you're stalking her.

How else would you have found her?"

"I found her because I know my way around technology far better than those old geezers attempting to keep her away from me. Once she came back to Seattle, it was easy to follow her out."

"You do realize you're the one with issues?" Jake asked. "Any normal person would have let her go."

"You know so much about me because…how? You've spent so much time with me? Or you've believed a liar?"

"I'm not a liar!" She crawled closer to Jake.

Trent turned to her. "Tiffany, you always have been, and you always will be. I'm the only one who accepts you the way you are. That's why you need to come back home with me." He jumped up and moved toward her.

Jake grabbed Trent's arm. "Don't go near her."

"Leave us alone. I need to deal with my wife." He shook free, and Jake scrambled to catch up. He shoved Trent, who turned around and glared at him. "I'll give you one last chance to walk away. Otherwise, you're going to regret ever meeting Tiffany."

"I'll never feel that way. She's the best thing to ever happen to me."

"Except that she's my *wife*. She promised to stay with me until death in front of hundreds of witnesses."

Elena…Tiffany…glared at Trent. "We're only married because divorce papers take time."

"That, and I'm never going to sign them."

"There are ways around that." She punched him.

Trent only laughed. "You think that hurts?" He turned to Jake. "Isn't she adorable?"

"I told you to escape," Jake said to her. "I'll deal with him."

She shook her head. "He's my problem, not yours." She turned to Trent. "I'm never going back with you. You're cruel, and I'm not putting up with it another moment. I hate you."

"You think I'm mean? Wow, you're even more stupid than I thought possible. I'm pointing out reality so you can change. I'm helping you become a better person."

Tears filled her eyes. "No, you're not. That's not how you help someone. Believing in them—that's how."

The hurt in her face ripped Jake's heart apart. He wrapped his fingers around Trent's neck, and squeezed as hard as he could. "Get out of here before I have to hurt you."

Trent grabbed his wrists and pulled Jake's hands away from his neck. "You? Hurt me?" He shook his head. "She needs me. Tiffany won't survive without me, and she knows it. That's why she was dumb enough to let me find her." He shoved Jake, and then grabbed Tiffany's arm.

She let out a cry of pain.

"Come on. We're going home, where you belong."

He shoved her, forcing her to walk. Each time she stepped on her bad leg, she limped and cried out again. "Shut up, Tiff." He slapped her.

Anger tore through Jake. No wonder she was on the run—this guy needed to be stopped. He pulled out his phone and dialed 911. As soon as there was an answer, he interrupted the dispatcher. "My girlfriend and I are being attacked. Send help immediately." He explained which beach they were at, and then ended the call.

Jake ran toward Trent at full speed, slamming into his back. The force caused him to let go of Tiffany. She stumbled to the ground, grasping her ankle. Trent turned around glared at Jake. "You're going to regret that, pansy boy."

"You think I'm scared of you? All you are is a bully. You pick on someone that once loved you—you're weak."

Trent's eyebrows came together. "Weak? You're the scrawny one, you scrawny—"

Jake punched him across the face. Trent stared at him for a moment before grabbing Jake's shoulders. Trent shoved him to the ground, hitting Jake in the face. He moved to do it again, but Jake blocked his fist.

"Stop," Tiffany cried.

From the corner of his eye, Jake saw Trent's other fist coming at his face. Jake raised his leg, kneeing Trent in the crotch. Trent's eyes widened, and a gasp escaped his mouth. Jake moved away from Trent while he had the chance. He ran over to Tiffany, and helped her up. "We've got to get you out of here."

"Your face." She rubbed a sore spot where Trent had punched him.

"I'm fine. Come on." They took a few steps, and then Jake heard the sound of sand crunching from behind. Trent wasn't going to give up, was he? Jake thought he heard sirens in the distance. He turned around in time to see Trent's fist make contact with his nose. Warm liquid ran down his mouth.

"Trent, stop!" Tiffany pleaded.

Pain shot through Jake's jaw when Trent slammed his fist into it.

"Only when you agree to come home where you belong," Trent said. "That's when I'll stop." He hit Jake again across the face, and Jake fell to the ground.

"Okay. I'll go, Trent." Tiffany limped toward him.

Jake turned toward her. "No! You can't. You won't survive."

She shook her head, tears shining in her eyes. "It's not worth it. You don't deserve this." Tears spilled down her cheeks.

Jake stood, moved to wipe her tears, but instead turned toward Trent, and hit him in the eye. "You don't deserve her, Trent, and you know it. The only reason you treat her bad is because in your sick mind, you think it'll make her stay with you. How'd that work for you?"

Trent's eyes narrowed, and suddenly, Jake flew to the ground, Trent landing on top of him. Jake's back became wet from water splashing around him. Trent rose to his knees over Jake, and then grabbed Jake's collar, dragging him to where the water was deeper. Jake gagged, trying to remove Trent's hands.

Tiffany yelled something, but Jake couldn't hear anything other than the water getting into his ears.

"This is how it's going to end." Trent shoved Jake's face into the water. His nose burned, and everything went quiet as the water covered his head. Jake tried screaming, but practically no sound escaped, and all he ended up with was water in his mouth. He kicked and grabbed at Trent, finally able to pull his face out of the water.

Jake gasped for air while still fighting Trent.

Trent scowled. "Don't worry. After I've taken care of you, Tiffany's coming home with me, and I'll treat her exactly as she deserves. She'll learn never to walk away from a real man ever again." He forced Jake under the water again. Everything went quiet again, and Jake fought harder. His lungs felt like they would explode, and terror ran through him. He needed air, but he wouldn't be able to fight off Trent much longer.

Then Tiffany would be forced to go home with that jerk.

Jake felt a rush of energy, and he managed to push his head up out of the water. He gasped for air again, his lungs burning. This time, he saw Tiffany walking into the water toward them. She screamed at Trent, hitting him in the back when she reached them.

Trent ignored her, and shoved Jake under again, but with less force. Jake managed to push himself up again, but fear tore through him when he looked over. Trent had his other hand wrapped around Tiffany's neck. She fought him, but he was slowly forcing her toward the water, too. Jake screamed, though it wasn't much after fighting for air under water.

Trent looked over at Jake. "Would you drown already?" He let go of Tiffany, shoving her away, and then used both hands to force Jake back under.

Jake grabbed Trent's arms, kicked at his torso while fighting to get out of the water. White dots danced in Jake's vision. He didn't have much time left. Through the silence, he brought his knees toward his chest, readying himself for one final kick. He had to break free, or he wouldn't survive—and neither would Tiffany.

He kicked with all his might. Stars continued to dance in his vision, but he saw Trent fly backwards. He broke free.

Jake found the ground, steadied his feet, and then sprung to the surface. He gasped, choked, and spit water out.

Trent splashed a few feet away until he managed to stand. His eyebrows furrowed, and he held a fist up toward Jake, shouted profanities and insults, and charged toward him.

Jake moved closer to Tiffany. Pain shot though his foot as he stepped on a sharp stick. He held his breath, dipped under the water, and pulled it up. It was long, a couple inches thick, and covered with short, prickly stubs. He kept it under the water so Trent wouldn't see it.

"Why don't you go back home?" Jake shouted. "Tiffany doesn't want anything to do with you."

"Doesn't matter. She's my wife." Trent lunged for Jake's neck, but Jake pulled out the stick and swung it across Trent's face. It left several scratches.

Trent tried to grab the stick, but Jake pulled it away. He hit Trent in the arm, digging the points in as far as possible. Trent swung at the stick, missing.

Tiffany rushed at Trent, shoving him in the back. Jake used his other arm to help her push him. He kicked Trent's knee, and he stumbled, falling into the water. Tiffany wrapped her hands around his neck, forcing him under.

"Take that," she shouted, continuing to hold him.

Trent grabbed at her arms, and Jake dropped the stick. He pushed Trent's arms away from Tiffany.

He turned to Tiffany. "Let go."

"What?"

"Not like this." Jake let go of Trent, and then so did Tiffany. Trent jumped up, gasping for air. Two police officers ran toward the water, shouting something Jake couldn't hear over Trent's splashing and sputtering. He turned his back on Trent, trying and failing to listen to the officers, and then turned back just in time to see Trent grope for him. Jake stepped back, out of his reach, and the police splashed beside him. They pulled him by his shirt, dragging him out of the water.

Jake took Tiffany's hand, and they made their way to the beach.

"Are you okay?" the officer asked.

Tiffany wrapped her arms around Jake, burying her face into his chest. She shook as she held him.

"Let's get you two to the ambulance," the officer said. "We'll ask you some questions while the medics check you out."

Tiffany leaned against Jake as they walked across the beach toward the flashing lights. Jake continued gasping for air between coughing up water. Tiffany kept looking at him, giving him looks of apology. As if any of this had been her fault.

Jake looked around for Trent. He was still near the shore, and now he was in handcuffs. The two cops near him appeared to be questioning him. Jake let out a sigh of relief.

When they reached the parking lot, he and Tiffany were led into the ambulance. They each sat on a bench across from each other. A medic examined her ankle while another checked Jake's breathing. Once they ascertained that his lungs were in good working order, they moved to his face.

"That's a deep wound, but it won't need stitches. Let's get it cleaned out so it doesn't get infected."

Once he and Tiffany were finally done, officers separated them for questioning. Jake still had trouble breathing, but managed to answer all of their questions.

When they were finally allowed to see each other, Jake ran to Tiffany, who now had crutches and a wrapped ankle. He threw his arms around her and held her tight. She leaned her head onto his shoulder, sobbing.

"Are you okay?" he asked, kissing the top of her head.

She looked up at him. "I'm so sorry, Jake. I'll never forgive myself."

Jake shook his head. "It's not your fault. I'm just glad you're safe."

"He almost killed you." She ran her fingers along his face.

Jake winced at the pain of her light touch.

"Just look at what he did to you." She frowned.

"I don't care. It's worth it knowing you're safe. I told you I would protect you."

Her eyes shone with tears. "I'm so sorry about lying to you about my name."

"Nonsense. You didn't lie—you just told me your new name."

"Still, I should have told you."

Jake kissed her nose. "Don't worry about silly details. It's an honor to spend time with you. I do have one question, though."

Tiffany looked nervous. "What?"

"Do you want me to call you Elena or Tiffany?"

She looked relieved. "What do you want to call me?"

"I want to call you whatever you want to go by."

She swallowed. "Well, I guess I don't need a new identity now. Do you like Tiffany?"

"I think it's beautiful. Just like you." He pulled her closer, and then placed his lips on hers. She relaxed in his arms and kissed him back, wrapping her arms around him while balancing on the crutches.

Thirty

Tiffany set the napkin on her plate. "Thank you so much for such a delicious meal." She looked at Dawn, Jake's mom, and smiled. "It was so good, I overate."

Several of Jake's brothers around the table laughed.

"It happens often," Brayden said, rubbing his stomach. "We all have to go on diets after coming back home."

"What are you going to do now, though?" Tiffany asked him. "Since you're living in Kittle Falls?"

Brayden looked thoughtful. "That's a good question. I suppose I'll have to stay on a diet at home and work, and then throw it all out the window when I come here to eat."

"Every day?" Dawn asked, winking.

"Good luck with that," Cruz said. "Mom's going to fatten us both up now that we're back home."

"Stop teasing your mom," Robert, their dad said. "I'm sure if you ask nicely, she'll make healthy meals. We're just glad the two of you are moving back to Kittle

Falls."

"Now we just need to work on you two." Dawn turned to Rafael and Zachary.

"Oh, we'll convince them," Brayden said. "Just wait and see."

"When is your grandpa coming back down?" Robert asked. "Now that I know how to play poker, he needs to come back so I can beat him."

Tiffany smiled. "I'll have to call him and ask. He had such a great time visiting."

"We'll have to work on moving him here, too," Cruz said, looking at Rafael.

"I'm not moving from LA," Rafael said, "but I do plan on visiting more often. I promise. I've been back more since Dad was in the hospital, right?"

"Yes, you have," Dawn said. "And we couldn't be happier." She turned to look at Zachary, who was busy typing on his laptop.

Brayden pretended to cough, and said, "Zachary."

He looked up. "What?"

Everyone laughed.

Jake leaned over to Tiffany. "Poor Zach has always been lost in his own world. It's part of what makes him a great writer, though."

"Are you moving back to town?" Cruz asked, ruffling Zachary's hair.

"Sorry. I'm staying in New York. One of these days, I'm going to get a big publishing deal. Then I'll fly you all over for a big celebration."

"You can write from anywhere," Brayden said. "You know that, right?"

Zachary rolled his eyes at Brayden. "Of course. But my agent thinks I'll have a better chance if I can meet someone in one of the publishing houses. She's setting up a meeting for early next year."

"Just think about it," Robert said. "Your mom and I would love nothing more than to have all our boys back home."

"One day," Zachary said, turning back to his laptop.

"Are you excited about working in the hospital?" Tiffany asked Brayden.

He frowned. "No, but it's only temporary. I'm going to use the money from selling my practice in Dallas to start a new one locally. Another thought I have is to open an urgent care facility here in Kittle Falls. Whenever anyone gets hurt, they have to travel a half an hour to the hospital. There are a lot of broken bones and other emergency situations."

"Heart attacks, too?" Tiffany asked.

"More than you'd imagine," Brayden said. "I'd love to help the town by starting an urgent care practice. We could also have a few smaller practices in the building, such as my cardiology clinic. If I could get a two or three more doctors to join me, we could make this happen." His eyes lit up.

"Oh, Brayden," gushed Dawn. "I couldn't be

prouder of you."

"Mom." Brayden looked away. "Stop."

The brothers all exchanged good-natured conversation for a few more minutes before everyone helped clear the table.

With so many people cleaning the kitchen, it sparkled in a matter of minutes. It never ceased to amaze Tiffany, and she loved every minute spent with the large family. She'd always dreamed of being part of an actual family, and now she knew what it felt like.

Jake's brothers all grabbed their winter coats and headed outside for a game of basketball in the driveway.

Robert came over to them. "I've never properly thanked either one of you for all your help with the shop." He looked into Jake's eyes. "You really went above and beyond the call of duty. And for that, we can't ever thank you enough, can we, hon?"

Dawn came over, and took Robert's hand. "No. Jake, we were unfair to you. You were grieving the loss of Sophia every bit as much as us. We shouldn't have expected—"

"Demanded," Robert said.

Dawn nodded. "We shouldn't have demanded that you take on all the work. Not when you needed the break as much as we did. And we want to make it up to you. Think of it as payment, plus interest."

Jake looked over at Tiffany, and they exchanged a look.

Robert cleared his throat. "Son, we've set up a fund for you. When you're ready to purchase a home, we have a generous down payment for you."

Jake looked back and forth between his parents. "Are you sure? You don't have to."

"Yes, we do." Dawn's eyes filled with tears. "We're so sorry for the way we treated you."

"Oh, Mom. Dad." Jake wrapped his arms around both of them. They hugged him tight, and Tiffany couldn't help getting teary at the sight.

Dawn and Robert stood back. He patted Jake on the shoulder. "Your mom and I are going to the shop to check on Bella and Calvin. They deserve a bonus as well." Robert winked at Tiffany, took his wife's hand in his, and then they headed outside.

Jake turned to Tiffany. "Can you believe that? A down payment on a house?"

Tiffany slid her arm through his. "All your hard work paid off. You're going to make some lucky girl very happy one day." She gave him a playful grin and then ran out of the room.

He chased after her, catching her halfway down the hall. He wrapped his arms around her, pulling her close. "Gotcha. You lose."

Tiffany nestled closer. "Actually, I think I won." She kissed his cheek, lingering where the stitches had been. There wasn't even a mark thanks to the creams she'd given him. "Want to watch a movie?"

"I'd love to." They went into the living room, and Jake turned on the TV as Tiffany got comfortable on the couch. The news came on, and Trent's ugly mug showed front and center. Jake turned the channel as quickly as he could, hoping Tiffany hadn't seen it.

"Turn it back," she said. "I want to hear what they have to say."

"You do?" He turned the station back to where it was, and then sat next to her. They held hands as they listened.

Trent's face remained on the screen. The two newscasters discussed his jail sentence. "Trent Saunders is facing life in jail for a lengthy list of felonies. The two charges of attempted murder in Kittle Falls are only the beginning. In Seattle, he's being charged with the attempted murder of Alfy Petosa, forgery, counterfeiting, tax fraud, aggravated assault, and finally, grand larceny."

Tiffany looked over at Jake. She tried to take in everything the newscasters had said. Had Trent done all that while they were married? Why hadn't she known that he was involved in so much wrongdoing? How could she have not realized what danger she had been in?

"He's going to jail for a long, long time," Jake said, pulling some stray hair behind her ear. "You don't have to worry about him anymore. I'd be surprised if he gets out before he's old and gray."

She looked into Jake's eyes, butterflies dancing in her stomach. Even though they'd seen each other every day for months, he still had that effect on her. She ran her fingers through his hair. "Not only that, but I have you now. I couldn't ask for anything more."

He held up her hand, adjusting the sparkling diamond engagement ring. "Me neither." He pulled her close and placed his lips on hers. Tiffany wrapped her arms around him, kissing him back.

Everything was going to be okay. No, more than that…it was going to be perfect.

Meet the Hunter brothers of Kittle Falls...

Seaside Surprises: *Jake, the heartbroken son who never left Kittle Falls*

Seaside Heartbeats: *Brayden, the successful cardiologist*

Seaside Dances: *Zachary, the struggling writer*

Seaside Kisses: *Rafael, the disillusioned fashion designer*

Seaside Christmas: *Cruz, the wild tattoo artist*

Sign up for book updates.
http://stacyclaflin.com/newsletter/

Other books by Stacy Claflin

The Transformed Series

Deception (#1)

Betrayal (#2)

Forgotten (#3)

Silent Bite (#3.5)

Ascension (#4)

Duplicity (#5)

Sacrifice (#6)

Destroyed (#7) – Coming Soon

Hidden Intentions (Novel)

A Long Time Coming (Short Story)

Fallen (Novella)

Taken (Novella)

Gone Trilogy

Gone

Held

Over

The Complete Trilogy

Dean's List (Standalone) – Coming Soon

Visit StacyClaflin.com for details.

Sign up for new release updates.
http://stacyclaflin.com/newsletter/

Join My Book Hangout:
facebook.com/groups/stacyclaflinbooks

to participate in fun bookish discussions. There are also exclusive giveaways, sneak peeks, and more. Sometimes the members offer opinions on book covers, too. You never know what you'll find!

65993856R00150